# Jessie's Flight to
## *Freedom*

*by*
Barbara Neveau

PublishAmerica
Baltimore

© 2006 by Barbara Neveau
All rights reserved. No part of this book may be reproduced, stored in a retrieval system or transmitted in any form or by any means without the prior written permission of the publishers, except by a reviewer who may quote brief passages in a review to be printed in a newspaper, magazine or journal.

First printing

At the specific preference of the author, PublishAmerica allowed this work to remain exactly as the author intended, verbatim, without editorial input.

ISBN: 1-4241-2414-X
PUBLISHED BY PUBLISHAMERICA, LLLP
www.publishamerica.com
Baltimore

Printed in the United States of America

# Chapter One

When I first got the news that Jessie was fighting cancer, I knew that I needed to be there. Lorrie O'Brien is my name and I have had the privilege of spending final precious time with my mentor and good friend Jessie Jonas. When I first called and asked Jessie if I could spend a few days with her she refused, saying that she was too busy getting her affairs in order to have guests. Thank God Samuel and Seth kept me informed of Jessie's failing health and each time I heard from them they told me that she was slowly wasting away. I called and begged Jessie to allow me to come and be of some help and comfort but she still said no, not yet. Well, I thought, at least she had said not yet this time. That must mean she was almost finished with her earthly tasks and ready for her appointment with death. Seth and Samuel called to say that Jessie had taken to her bed and they felt uncomfortable with the task of taking care of her bodily needs. They obviously thought the time of death was very near.

When I stood at Jessie's bedroom door and saw her gaunt face peeping out from under the quilt that Sadie had given her, I wanted to cry but didn't dare. I couldn't believe how tragically my friend had changed physically. Her once ample body was barely making a mound beneath the covers. She was shaking with spasms from the cold chills that were attacking her body. That display of uncontrolled weakness from such a gutsy lady made me thankful that I had come when I did. I prayed that I hadn't come too late; did she have any strength left?

This small frail woman on the bed was not the Jessie who Sadie, Kate, Harrison and I had known and loved. When I first met Jessie she was a human dynamo, she could create a scrumptious meal out of bare essential, she could control a house full of prostitutes with tolerance, love, and more importantly respect.

As I watched from the doorway my mind went back to Haven Place and the good times we had shared. My God how strong she is even in the face of death. I love this woman who was lying on the bed holding her sides shaking with laughter from something funny Seth had told her. Even while suffering from this horrible pain, this woman, my friend Jessie is a tower of strength. When I entered her bedroom she smiled through her pain and said, "I was hoping you would come."

She had finally given up her struggle against cancer and had been bedridden for two days when Samuel called to tell me of her condition. That was the signal that I was waiting for. I grabbed the bags that had been packed for weeks, kissed my husband and teen aged daughter and boarded the train from Buffalo to New York City, and my friend's side.

Seth was trying to keep from showing his grief by repeating funny stories that had happened at the restaurant. Jessie had always enjoyed the antics that some of her few difficult customers performed while pretending to be superior to the folks that waited on them.

I watched as a momentary frown flashed on the tiny face. She was masking the pain that tore through her body. My admiration soon reached new heights in that first week that I spent caring for Jessie.

She clearly was so near death that her black skin had turned a brownish gray and yet she laughed, teased and continued to rule the roost.

Kate who had given the black boys, Seth and Samuel, their freedom immediately after Harrison had purchased them, had asked Jessie to take them under her wing until they learned to live, as freed men. Jessie had not only agreed to take them under her wing, but she had also taken them into her heart. She treated both boys as the sons she never had and even now they were her mainstay, although she wouldn't admit it.

Seth and Samuel, the boys, had made their home with Jessie through the years. The boys were always devoted to her, but Jessie needed a women and lifelong friend to be with her during her last few days on earth.

I noticed right away that her manner of speech had changed, she now talked just as fine as others, but I kept my own council. I wondered if she had hired a tutor, or had she attend a special school for adults? I didn't know. I did know that when she was ready to tell me about her change in speaking, nothing on earth could stop her.

That excruciating pain that comes with cancer had taken its toll on this once vibrant woman. She fought hard to hide her suffering, but I could still read the pain in her eyes. I hated seeing my friend this way, dying, no family members to mourn her. Jessie had spent most of her life waiting on others and now she was alone with only her friends to see her off. Jessie must have read my thoughts because she sat up and blustered out,

"You aren't feeling sorry for me are you? Why, I've had a good and exciting life. Oh, I've had some hard rows to hoe but time seems to iron out the bumps in life. What I've missed in my life ain't much to worry about."

Jessie, I apologized, I was just feeling bad that some of your family couldn't be here with you. I'm sorry.

"Don't be feeling sorry for me, I've had my real family in my heart all these years. Sadie is my adopted child and you and all the other gals at Haven Place are my sisters. My sons, Seth and Samuel, have been loyal and Kate and Harrison accepted and watched over me the same as any good parents would for as long as Kate lived. Harrison still keeps in contact with me each week so now you do see I've got me a family.

"My God I know my life wasn't pretty at first but it got better when I made it on my own. I've had a good life and I'm ready to pass on to that other place."

Jessie paused and with the saddest look I have ever seen on her usually smiling face, she added, "Maybe there they won't see color."

At first her face showed her despair, and then to my surprise she changed again. her whole manner took on a humorous, teasing air.

Grinning mischievously, she chuckled, "Girl, let me tell you about my early years and then you will see why I say that I've had a good and interesting life right up to the end of my days."

Jessie's eyes danced as she slowly eased back down on the bed, her safe, warm springboard for pleasant memories, and she began again.

"Miz Tilda was a little old Negro woman who helped all the other women deliver; they called her a mid-wife. Here's what Miz Tilda told me about the day I was born. She said that my Mama's screams filled the night air; her shrieks of pain had sprung from the small shack at the very end of a cluster of cabins that the white folks called Nigger Heaven. My mama was lying on a cot holding a screaming baby. That was me. Tilda said that room was small and dark just like me. She swore to me that every time a child was born in that sweltering room with its one bare cot and broken down rocker, reeking of fear, pain, and death, that it became a silent monument to the resilience and the courage of all black women.

"My mama was a golden skinned girl and that's the color that the master liked best. Tilda said she remembers thinking, how my mama's whole women parts was ripped to hell an gone giving life to a half-breed child that ain't gonna have no life, no how. She said it don't seem right, children forced to have children and no say in it anyhow."

"Miz Tilda explained that she had to force her mind back to the present and to the job of trying to stem the blood flowing from my mama. Lissie was Mama's name and she was but a child herself. She was the thirteen-year-old concubine of Master Jessie Jonas.

"Miz Tilda asked my mama what she was going to call her child that she brought into this land of misery. She was just trying to give Mama something to think about beside the pain that came after delivering the master's bastard.

"Miz Tilda, I gonna call her Jessie, after Mr. Jessie Jonas, her daddy. God help me, I don't care who knows she's Mr. Jessie's child, and maybe then he take her and give her a better life."

"Don't no white man want a black child wearing his name. You say that child is his and he should claim her, but that don't mean he will," Miz Tilda had warned Mama. Shaking her head, Miz Tilda said she sat back down in the rickety old rocker, puffing on her corncob pipe while she debated how to further caution Mama in how dangerous it was naming a child after its white father. After she had finally stopped the flow of blood Miz Tilda packed my mama's torn body with rags that she had boiled just for that event. Miz Tilde watched as Mama slipped off to sleep and a land where pain was bearable. Miz Tilda said she used that precious free time to daydream away the long hours of rest that were needed by any mother after a long, hard delivery."

"Miz Tilda told me she remembered thinking, *the child Lissie just needs rest an she be all right.* She had tried to reassure herself. *cain't have another child dying cause thet bastard cain't keep his dinghy in his pants!*

Jessie chuckled and explained to me, "When I got older and learned to read I wondered, what the hell is a dinghy, when I looked the word up in the dictionary it said it was a small boat that saves lives. Ain't no way those white men's dinghy saved our lives."

"Lorrie honey, the way that Miz Tilda described the room, I could smell the sweat and blood, and I could almost see the dust that was floating in the strip of sunlight that was cutting its way into that gloomy room. She said it also it was almost peaceful as Mama slept and she sat rocking me, daydreaming of freedom. I stirred in my sleep and Miz Tilda said she took me to the side of the cot where Mama lay. She said my mama opened her arms even though she was still half asleep and she pressed me close to her side. She said the morning sun came bursting into the shack as the door was thrown open by Joseph, the old black butler, his face frozen in fear. Master of the plantation, Master Jessie Jonas marched over to the cot where Mama lay trembling.

"I hear tell you claiming I'm that thing's daddy. That sure ain't no part of me! You were sneaking out with that no account Hoagie. That thing looks just like him, as black as the ace of spades. He stared down at me snuggled in my Mama's arms and shouted, don't let me ever hear of you saying that's my child, you hear? Now you laid in that bed long enough, get yourself out to the fields, Tilda can watch over that,…that thing. "

"He called me a thing, imagine that!" Jessie chuckled as she recalled the past, "no matter, I heard he got his later"

"Can't I have a few more hours?" My mama had begged.

"Her pleading fell on stone ears. Miz Tilda said he went prancing out of the birthing cabin shaking his bald head, rubbing his big gut and complaining about lazy niggers and their loose and careless ways.

"Miz Tilda told me that all the black folks standing in the yard heard him and that some of the men spit as the Master walked by but he was too peeved to notice.

"Handing me to Tilda, Mama made a grand effort to stand. Bright red blood gushed from her as she tried to follow her master's command. She sank back down on the cot, the effort to obey had left her weak and dazed.

"Miz Tilda put me on the rocker and again tried to stop the flow of blood as Mama Lissie lay with her life force draining from her weakened body. Miz Tilda took on a sad face and told me the room was suddenly washed with the sweet sickening smell of death. Just then Miz Tilda said I let out an ear piercing scream, she said it was almost as if I knew that my mother was dying.

"Joseph had hurried back into the shack pressing his finger against his lips, cautioning Mama and Miz Tilda to hush and don't cause any trouble as the master's wife was outside. Miz Tilda tearfully whispered that my mama, little Lissie wouldn't cause any more trouble, as she was dead! She was dead cause that white man cain't keep his hands off the young ones, she had at hissed at Joseph. Mama was only seen thirteen years old and now she was dead from giving birth to a white man's bastard.

"Miz Tilda remembered that when the door swung open and the face of

Mrs. Jonas peeped into the gloomy room, that bitch with the pincheyed up nose and squinty eyes took in everything at a glance. My mama dead on the bed, me tightly wrapped, lying in the chair and Tilda and Joseph huddled together in the corner of the shack fearing what might come next.

"Humph," was the sound that came out of her chicken neck as she cleared her throat. "Well, another low life dying from consorting with various men! When will you people learn? You don't see white folks lying abed with everything that takes their fancy! Come Joseph…I need my afternoon tea."

"Miz Tilda said Joseph just rolled his eyes and followed the Mistress toward the house.

"Shore we see it," Tilda had raged "they're like the animals they say we are, they are stealing our young girls bodies, forcing them to their beds, using them like brood mares………More babies, more workers."

"Taking me from the chair, she had made her way to her own shack at the very end of the row. She had moved there three years ago when the master decided she was too old to work the fields. Miz Tilda said the only reason he hadn't sold her is that no one would pay the price the master was asking.

"The closer, larger, shacks were for the field hands and who ever they were living with at the time. The Master never permitted marriage between his slaves; it would cause too much trouble when and if he wanted to sell one or both.

"Master Jessie was one of those slave owners that believed that the black man was less than an animal and that is the way they should be treated. What does that tell you about a man who thinks it's all right to have relations with supposed animals?"

"There was never any problem for him when it came to selling the children, they all belonged to him whether they did or not and were sold whenever he needed money. He had once explained to a neighbor his theory behind the selling of the little ones, and Miz Tilda had heard him bragging to the neighbor about how he enjoyed the favors of the young golden girls. When she got a belly full of child he traded her for a fresh young one.

"Oh sure," he had bragged, "the women whine for a while when I sell one of their pica ninnies but they soon get over it and then they pop out another one. These darkies breed like rabbits."

"What the Master didn't know is that secret ceremonies were often performed when two people decided to pledge to each other. Jumping over the broom handle was just as binding to the couple as the wedding ceremony was to the white people.

*JESSIE'S FLIGHT TO FREEDOM*

"Miz Tilda said both the men and the women tried to keep from having children cause the likelihood of their offspring being sold away tore at their hearts. Nature being what it is, there were children born and children died, but the biggest fear was the cruel separation for the children that comes from being torn away from parents who loved them That fear lit a fire that lay smoldering in the breast of every man, woman, and child on the plantation.

"Even after the master had taken me away from her, Miz Tilda spent many a night telling me the stories of my birth and the goings on around the plantation. She said that was the only way that people would someday know the whole story. Most black folks couldn't read nor write. It wasn't allowed, so if we didn't tell the stories over and over we would soon forget. But let me get back to my account now while I can still think clearly."

"After Joseph had served the mistress her tea and biscuits, washed and polished the silver tea set and placed it back on the sideboard so all could admire it. Madam always liked her silver displayed on red velvet runners, it made the silver look even richer.

"Now, having had her appetite slaked and still feeling empty and unsatisfied she sat and waited for her cold, indifferent husband to come home to her. She heard the sounds of his horse clomping up the hardened dirt path in front of the house. She jumped to her feet and had fleeting thoughts about running to the front door to wait. Maybe today he would see her affection and return it; maybe today he would hold her like he did when they were courting. Her instinct told her that today would not be the day to be waiting near the front door, not with all the excitement of Lissie's death so fresh in his mind. He did so hate to lose another slave especially one so young. Lissie had owed many more years of work to her master and by dying she had cheated Jessie out of his bought and paid for property. He was going to be in a vile mood and she had better sit back and wait.

"Sissy Jonas, Master's wife of ten lonely years, took a seat on the divan at the far end of the front hall while she waited for her husband to enter the door. She had begun her married life rushing to meet him at the end of the day but his cold behavior and the meanness he sometimes used while shoving her away soon stopped that practice, now she waited a safe space away to see what kind of mood he was in before she came within swinging distance.

"Mr. Jessie Jonas was proud of his foyer and as he crossed the length of it to stand before his trembling wife, Joseph had heard Master begin grumbling. What in hell is she going to whine about now? Sissy is always whining about something. Christ, how I hate that name, 'Sissy,' what the hell kind of name is that for a grown woman?"

"Miz Jonas had nervously asked her husband if he knew that Lissie girl had died in childbirth. And Sissy had explained to the master that she was just about ask Lissie to move into the house. She would have made and excellent upstairs maid.

"Honestly, Jessie, sometimes I think those people do these things on purpose just to make life miserable."

"Joseph later told Miz Tilda that the master turned on his wife, grabbed the front of her dress, lifted her from the divan and viciously began to pound her. He then shoved her against the wall.

"You mean to tell me you think Lissie died just to upset your plans?" He shouted, "Woman, are you an idiot? She died because she was weak and foolish. Those kind need us to take care of them and when we don't they die."

"Having set his stupid wife straight Jessie climbed the stairs to his office. He had to record the death of Lissie and to figure the cost of replacing her.

"Too bad the baby was a puny female; I won't get half the price of a healthy boy child. It's just too bad that sweet young thing, Lissie had to die, oh well replace her and forget it.

"Good God Joseph, I work hard all day long trying to give my family the very best and this is the thanks I get for it. No wonder a man has to go far a field for comfort in the bed. That wife of mine and her constant whining would drive a man insane," Master Jonas had complained

"Tilda said that that evil old man treated Joseph as though he didn't have any thoughts about the misuse of the girl children, as though Master was God and Joseph was without a soul."

" Joseph always came down to have tea with Miz Tilda after the household jobs were done, they would sit and gossip about the goings on in the house. One night he was laughing so hard he could hardly talk. He said Master Jonas had been reminiscing about the good old days and then he told Joseph how he had come about marrying Sissy.

"She was damned lucky her pappy had all that money when he died or she would have been a spinster for life. Not many men are brave enough to marry a woman with a face like a prune and a disposition to match. She ain't a trollop but she might as well be, always complaining that I don't give her enough of my time. A man can't diddle that in the daylight, and at night I'm too tired!

"That child that came out from Sissy ain't what a man wants for an heir," Master Jonas had confided to Joseph, "A man needs a clever son to carry on his father's name, not a babbling idiot. Maybe if I can arrange a proper marriage and if the wife has a few brains along with money we will have a grandson to carry on the proud name of Jonas."

"Travis, son of Jessie and Sissy Jonas, looked like his mother, blond hair, fair skin and the weirdest yellow eyes, but his temperament was that of his father. Even at an early age he had treated the slaves on his father's property as subjects for his entertainment. He beat the smaller boys with sticks and the girls were his special objects of tortured. They were forced to suck on his small penis while he held them by their ears. Needless to say the children all disappeared when Travis was loose on the grounds."

"As the Master sat recording his cost for his household, he complained about having to wait for the next auction. Two more days until Saturday and the next slave sale in town, it was going to be a long two days, but he would make up for it when he bought the new gal.

"He confided his ugly thoughts to Joseph as though, he was thinking out loud. *I suppose I could give Sissy a go tonight. Christ, am I really that hard up or just horny as hell from seeing Lissie on that cot all hot and sweaty?"*

"He actually told Joseph of his sick pipe dreams, how he wished for a place where beautiful light skinned slave girls knelt at his feet begging for his attention.

"You know Lorrie, it didn't pay to be a pretty child if you was black in the south, you got chosen by some white man and didn't even have a say in it."

Jessie's bitterness washed over me like a suffocating cloud of grief. I touched my friend's wrinkled cheek as the tears ran down my own.

Jessie why don't you rest for a while and then we can talk some more later, I asked.

"What if there isn't any later?" Jessie questioned, "If you don't want to hear my story just say so."

"Oh by the way did I tell you about the strange happening at the plantation? Travis, the Master's son disappeared from the house one hot day and was later found floating in the pond That pond was way over the ridge from where the workers were picking or they would have been blamed. There was a good deal of mourning from the folks in the big house but relief from the children in the slave quarters."

Dear friend, I didn't want to hurt you, I'm just worried about your getting too tired.

"I know child, I am being cantankerous in my old age, not like my sweet natured self of the past," snickered Jessie until she began to cough and thrash violently around the bed.

I went to her and bathed her sweaty face and neck with camphor; I found the violet scented lotion sitting on the bureau and pouring some of the liquid into my hands proceeded to smooth it on Jessie's feverish body, Jessie settled down and continued her life story.

"After the funeral the Master had decided that Tilda was too old to raise a child. He claimed that she was touched in the head, just because she went around mumbling to herself about the death of Travis and I was given to Cassie and George Washington Abrams to raise."

"Where we gonna put another child, can you answer me that?" Cassie Abrams had demanded. "We wall to wall children now."

"No my love," answered George Abrams, "I can't answer you as to where we will put another child, but you will figure out something, you always do."

"Sure, you nappy headed lover, leave it all to me like you always do," Cassie said as she kissed his mouth and ran her fingers through his tight gray curls,

"You gonna have to git that little George off this tit so the child can nurse, Master said we cain't have the goat for milk," George said as he squeezed one of Cassie's ample breasts.

"Dear Lord I gotta nourish another one of his bastards, when it gonna end? You know how I got me those other two and now I got Lissie's child. When that old man gonna let us alone? Every night I pray that his pecker will fall off, but it don't. And everyday there he is strutting around like a cock in a hen yard."

"God gonna get him for all his wrongs, he gonna end up in hell sure as anything" George promised.

"Dammit George, I want to be there to see it," raged Cassie.

"Cassie already had four children of her own, two by the Master and a boy and a girl by George Washington Abrams. She had been Master's sweet thing until she reached the age of sixteen and she was replaced with Pansy a lighter child of twelve. Cassie had laughed when she told Miz Tilda and George the secret of Pansy.

"That little gal Pansy was already loving Judi, that Judi be fourteen and

*JESSIE'S FLIGHT TO FREEDOM*

black as night, she from the Canfield Plantation. They meet at the corner of the south field and spend the night together. Mr. Jessie never will find much satisfaction from that one. When he finally gave up and replaced her, he sold her to Master Canfield. That little deal made Pansy and Judi very happy."

# Chapter Two

All the black folks knew who my father was; the only one who didn't was the Master's wife and I often wondered if she knew too, but denied it to herself.

"As soon as she thought I was old enough to understand, the frustrated Cassie explained why she was so full of bitterness toward me, but it didn't change the hurt and loneliness I had always felt. I just knew in my heart that I would be alone the rest of my life. Cassie told me what happened the day I came to live with them; as she explained it blow by blow to this four-year-old child, the emptiness began to build in my gut. I remember waking in the night with dreams of a giant white spider, huge body and long skinny arms and legs. It was always watching and waiting its chance to pounce on me. The first time I had the dream I woke up screaming. I was sent outside to the stoop and there I spent the rest of the night. It was the longest night of my life. I remember hearing every scratch and creak the world made. After that long and scary night, I did not cry out. Whenever I had that hateful dream, I put my left thumb in my mouth and put my other hand between my legs, that way I could lull myself back to sleep. I told myself I held my crotch to keep from peeing and getting the others wet, but the truth of the matter was it gave me a sense of being held and loved by someone."

"Right after the first time I had the dream and woke the others, Cassie wanted to give me to some other family, she said I wasn't right in the head, but master Jessie wouldn't permit it.

"Now Cassie," George had said, "we got to mind our own business, won't do much good to complain, the dirty work is done."

"So you say! You only have to work the fields; I gotta take care of all these children and still work the fields. Men have it easy!"

"You right Cassie," George sighed gently, "you always right,"

"From the time I was first learning to walk I heard comments from everyone around me especially from Cassie."

*JESSIE'S FLIGHT TO FREEDOM*

"Old Pinchynose gotta know who that child's daddy be," Cassie had complained, "he ain't hopping into her bed so she gotta know he getting it somewhere."

"Now Cassie you know we gotta mind our own business," George reminded her.

"So you say! You only have to work the fields; I gotta take care of all these children and still work the fields. Men have it easy!"

"You right Cassie," George sighed gently, "you always right,"

"If I heard Cassie say that once I heard her say that at least a hundred times a day, and George always answered the same way. It was if he was too tired to think of any thing else to say."

"The next few years flew as the Abrams family flourished. The work was hard but the nights after sundown were filled with love and companionship for most of the family. A good number of nights all the families would gather in front of the cabins and the children would play games, but on the nights when they were too tired to play the adults would tell stories of their mothers, their fathers, and the long ago home across the water.

"Dessie was Cassie and George's only daughter and thank God she was dark skinned, at least she would have a chance.

"On cold nights, I always had the space on the floor by the outside wall next to Dessie, so I could catch the cold breeze that blew through the cracks. I remember always being cold on one side and warm on the other, same as the hot nights, always sweating on the back from the heat that poured through those same cracks. Guess I was lucky, I had a home!"

"On the days that bad things happened the whole camp was quiet. You could always tell when another child had been took and used. The child was always froze up inside. The mama and daddy held them close, they couldn't say anything, but you could smell the hate growing".

"I watched as parents held their little ones knowing that someday that might be their child. The worst part is the knowing that you were measured less then human with no feelings or rights, and those sinful men thought that their actions was perfectly alright."

"Most often someone would start to hum an old hymn just to ease the pain, the separation from home, loved ones, and the ever-gnawing pain of being held captive.

"I loved the humming, still do today; it was the only thing that gave me a sense of belonging. I knew there was something different about me, but I didn't understand why. I always seemed to be standing on the outside of everything looking in, watching others having fun.

"I once ask Miz Tilda when I was born and she just shook her head and said I was born in the fall. Don't matter what day cause we never get to enjoy it anyhow!"

"When I turned about seven my safe world came to an end. The morning began as usual, up before dawn, eat a bowl of cornmeal mush, take off the nightdress pull on my burlap dress over bare body and head for the fields.

"I remember this special morning looking down at my brown legs, with a film of dust and spots where the pee had splashed back as I stood in the back of the cabin this morning and peed in the dust. Cassie was always reminding me too squat when I peed but it seemed like such a waste of time that I usually forgot and was splattered. Besides the boys got to stand and they weren't any better than me. Poop now that was another matter, you had to squat so you were close to the ground and the green grass and leaves that were used to wipe the mess from your hinder.

"This morning the Master's overseer, Jack, was waiting in the square where they always gathered waiting for the wagon to take them to the far fields. Jack herded us children into small group away from the parents.

"He announced, that all the children were going to market, and all the workers had better get to work in the west field. He reminded them that he would punish any slackers."

"Oh no, I thought, I should have listened to Miss Cassie and squatted when I peed, now their tired of telling me and their sending me away."

"The moans from the crowd started low in the back of the group and gathered momentum as the seconds ticked by.

"Women screamed, men tried to comfort them, while Jack stood with his gun drawn and pointed at the crowd.

David, the camp cripple died that morning! He had been beaten and then shot two years before while trying to escape to find his and Fannie's children. They had been sold the year before to a plantation owner in the next county and the anguished David ached to find them and bring them back to their mama.

Master Jessie had kept David around as an example for the others. When Jack had beaten David unmercifully, Master Jessie had proclaimed.

"See what you get when you disobey your master? You're lucky I didn't let him kill you!"

"I guess that David had heard that one too many times, that and Fannie's crying after lost children had set him crazy. He swore to fight the next sale of babies. Master Jessie wasn't any better then the other white folks, but at least they were with family who could love and try to protect them. I guess he had enough of the pain and humiliation of being treated like a piece of property. He attacked Jack the overseer.

As the gunshot reverberated through the cluster of cabins David was drawing his last breath.

"Fannie,…I love you…………Fannie honey, I'm free at last,………. freeee!

"Lorrie, I never will forget that howl of pain mixed with joy. In a way he had beaten Master Jessie."

"Terror must have torn at Fannie's heart causing her to cry out,

"Children gone, now David gone, what should I do? Will I be sold away from the only world I ever knew?"

"Running up to Jack, who was still holding the gun, she had dropped to her knees and wrapped her arms around his legs pleading for mercy.

"Please don't send me away. I'll be good, I'll work hard. I will do what ever you say so help me God!"

"Jack had lifted his leg and kicked her straight in the face, blood and teeth flew, and then he laughed. I saw that happen but didn't know why we were treated so badly, they never whipped their dogs or horses. I was too young to know that we were human too.

"Miz Tilda said she walked to the broken Fannie and helping her up, guided her toward the cabin where she and David had lived and tried to raise their three children.

"Don't waste your time going to that cabin," Jack had shouted, "you're out of there. We want somebody in that house that can work and earn his keep. Master Jonas gonna buy a new nigra to live in that fine place," Jack had taunted the wounded women.

"You come with me, there's plenty room in my place," Miz Tilda promised the frightened Fannie. Bending low Miz Tilda had whispered, how she hated hate that thing that calls himself a man,

"The crowd hurried away toward the fields as the two women stumbled toward Tilda's shack. The blood dripping from Fannie's broken face left a rusty trail in the dusty ground."

"You sure you want to hear the rest of this, it's a not a pretty picture, but it is a true story about being born black in the south?"

Yes my dear friend I do want to hear what happened in your life that made you so special to everyone who knew you." I answered.

"Can you picture the utter shame, the misery?" questioned Jessie.

" I will never forget that day; I was just about seven and had no idea that there was a different world out there. It took many twist and turns in my life to find a home and family, but I succeeded and I wouldn't trade a day of my life for any other. Well, maybe one, but that is another story. Back to the beginning."

"The overseer loaded us children on the flatbed trailer, Tommy; Master's stable boy came out of the barn leading a team of horses to the waiting Jack.

"Can't you just see us, frightened, crying children huddling together under a burning sun, holding on to each other on that old flatbed trailer?

"The howling seemed to make the overseer angry, and he bellowed, "Shut the hell up. He said we were going to a better place to work, we didn't have a chance here. If we were lucky some white man will buy us and let us work in their house. He reminded us that anything is better than working all our lives in the field and dying there."

"Jack threatened us with the whip and shouted, "Now quit your whining and settle down."

"Master always sold off the dark skinned little girls, as he preferred the high yellow or golden skinned females. Small, petite little girls with golden skin were his favorites, the younger the better. Any female child over ten would do.

"Jack always seemed pissed off when he had to do the master's dirty work and selling children was dirty work.

"I ain't much better than a slave on this place myself, he always complained to anyone who would listen, My papa sending me to Master Jonas when I was twelve years old sure looks the same as slaving to me. Papa gets to farm the north section, and for that privilege I was traded to Master Jonas. Lucky me. Sure, I get paid, but when Master figures out how much I owe for rent and food I'm always in debt to him. Can't figure out how I can eat more than I earn! If I could read than maybe I could figure out how that is."

"Maybe that is what made him so mean but folks didn't have any sympathy for that white boy; he didn't know what real slavery was."

"I was one of the children on the wagon and I was frozen with fear. Oh I knew that Master Jonas was my father but I didn't know what that really meant. Most of the other children lived with their parents, but I lived with George and Cassie. Being half grown and living with strangers didn't give an unhappy child many answers."

"We stood clutching each other and watching as Cassie fought George's hold on her; Cassie was screaming as Dessie, her only daughter was being taken to the trailer.

"Dessie and me huddled together, hugging each other with one arm and using the other to hang on to one of the wooden slats that acted like walls on the trailer. When the horses were hitched to the wagon, Jack hopped up to the wooden seat and hollered out to hang on cause he wasn't going to stop fer anything."

"My hand had slipped on the wooden side bar and I got a sliver of wood in the palm of my hand. It bled but I didn't feel the pain, I was numb with fright. I swore right then, that if I was ever to get free nobody was going to be in charge my life again.

"Oh, I knew that my Mama was dead but at the time I didn't really know what that meant either. I did know that Mama and Papa never came to see me but I didn't know why they hated me, maybe because I was ugly; all the other children said I was a half-breed. They all had different papas but they called me a half-breed. I always thought if I was pretty like Dessie, then maybe I would have parents that love me too.

"George pulled Cassie away from the trailer and flopping her over his shoulder he carried her into the cotton field, all the while gut-wrenching moans were ripping from his soul. George was just as frantic over the loss of his baby daughter. His woman still on his shoulder, he headed toward the far field where he and the others could freely vent their grief in the only way that they were permitted. We could hear the anguish and trapped fury in the singing, as Jack drove to town and the slave auction. Dessie was sold right away. She was frantic over being separated from me but she had no choice. The other children were slowly being sold and I was awestruck by the man who was auctioning us off. He talked so fast that I couldn't keep up with what he was saying. Why does he keep saying thirty, no forty, now fifty, and why were all those men checking our teeth and rubbing our arms and butts. I hated that when they put their fingers in my pee place and then my mouth to look at my teeth."

"The noon bell rang and the men that had gathered for the auction began drifting away with their new slaves, I looked around and saw that I was the only one left. The auctioneer shook his head and motioned for Jack to load me back on the trailer.

"Didn't nobody want me?" I asked.

"Hell no!" shouted Jack, "You ain't big enough to work and too small to bed. Why would anybody pay good money fer you?"

"Grabbing me roughly he tossed me back on the trailer, all the while swearing under his breath.

"What am I gonna do with you, I can't take you back to Master Jessie he gonna cut yer head off!"

"I remember that like it was yesterday. I sure didn't want my head cut off and I wasn't sure I wanted to be sold. I felt my dress getting wet from the pee that spilled out and leaked down my skinny little legs making tracks in the dust that covered my small body, and then I messed myself. Now I knew that Master Jessie was gonna kill me for sure. Looking around I spotted a wagon full of children headed in the opposite direction. Slipping off the slow moving wagon I ran for the other wagon as it passed the newspaper office. Catching hold of a slat on the side of the wagon I pulled myself up and joined the rest of the children.

"Jack must have pretended he didn't see me drop off the end of the wagon, cause then he wouldn't be responsible for another dead pica ninny. Master wouldn't dare whip him for losing a child; Master wouldn't want the other black folks to know that his overseer was as helpless as they were. Jack must have known that I was the master's child but he also knew he was a dead man if he said so.

"I could almost hear him say, "Ain't none of my affair, and couldn't change it even if I wanted to.

"I heard later that Master Jessie had beaten Jack anyway for losing a valuable piece of his property, but I'm sure in Master's mind he was probably glad the evidence of his misdeeds was gone. If he didn't see me, I didn't exist, besides he had his eye on that little half-breed girl on General Hopkins's place.

"The grapevine said that the General had mentioned to Jessie Jonas that he might sell Ramona as she was causing turmoil amongst the male slaves. When she had turned twelve, the tall slim Ramona became a beautiful women child and the General didn't have the heart to whip his slaves for the fighting over her.

"General Hopkins was in his eighties and the last of his line, his wife had been dead for ten years and they had not been lucky enough to have even one child to inherit this plantation. To the General's great disappointment the only family he had left was a distant nephew in Georgia and he was a no account rustler. The General's secret plan was to free the people he owned when he died and let the cousin rehire them if he wanted workers. The only one that knew where the freedom paper were hidden was Flora the cook. He couldn't make his plan known while he still lived, the other plantation owners would hang him for being disloyal to the south.

"The day that Jessie Jonas came to discuss the sale of Ramona, General Hopkins saw the lecherous look on Master Jessie's face and decided right then and there that the sale was off. Oh, he had heard the stories about owners violating their slaves, but he being an honorable man did not believe it, that is until now. The General vowed it would be a cold day in hell before that vile man would touch that sweet young thing.

"Jessie Jonas was angry but didn't dare show it, the General was highly respected and Jessie didn't want the other plantation owners to have to choose sides. He knew if they had to choose, he'd lose. Besides he was still under close scrutiny by the others for letting a slave child remain free for a whole week. He had pretended to search for me but he only halfheartedly investigated a few rumors of my whereabouts.

"She was probably dead from wild animals, he was heard to declare."

"Ramona also having heard the news on the plantation's human grapevine knew that she was in terrible trouble. The General was a kind man, but still a white man that could sell or trade her on impulse.

"According to Abe, the General's houseboy, Ramona's brother Tatro, who had been sold to the Franklin Farm, had run away and was hiding in the piney woods across the river.

"Mama, joining him will be easy," Ramona told her mother, "but hiding will be harder. Where will we sleep and where will our food come from? Mama, I'm scared of what might happen if I run, but I'm more scared of what's gonna happen if I stay."

"She saw Master Jessie leave and he didn't look happy. The General must have set too high a price for her. If Master Jessie did get his way in buying her, she was sure she would end up paying a far greater price.

"Gotta get away before he comes back," she told Abe, the generals house boy, "I don't trust that Master Jessie, I heard stories bout him."

"Won't do no good to run, he just bring you back and it be worse for you. I know what running is like; before I come here to this place, I hid for weeks in an old barn too scared to even search for food. I caught rats that come into the barn hunting food just like me. Shaking his head sadly, tears running down Abe's wrinkled old face, he continued.

"Rats and field mice don't taste so good but they kept me alive. It was worse then being owned by a master. When I wandered onto General Hopkins's farm he fed me and gave me a place to bed down. It was the best damn sleep I had all the time I was on the run."

"Well, you old, I'm young, maybe that be the difference." Ramona said, childishly patting his wrinkled old hand that lay in his lap.

She had made up her mind, she was gonna run, she later told me that she had decided, there ain't no white man gonna stick his nasty thing in her.

# Chapter Three

My futile attempt at escape had been in vain 'cause I had joined another batch of children headed for the sale block to be sold. As the wagon pulled up to the wooden platform where the slaves were paraded, I again slid off the back of the trailer and headed for the barn where the animals were held for auction. My luck was holding or maybe a small black girl with frightened eyes was a too common sight for anyone to notice.

"The noonday sun and the body heat from the few horses made the barn more oppressive, I crept into a stall, scraped together some straw and built myself a nest, I crawled into the wet moldy nest and fell asleep. I woke up wringing wet with sweat, my stomach was twisting into knots from hunger, but I was too scared to try to get away in the still fading light. My bottom was itching from the dried shit, and it seems I had also peed while in that deep sleep. Finding a pail of water near the door I washed my dress and myself then waited for dark to come. When night finally did come I hightailed it for the woods. I didn't know where I was going or what was out there, but to a seven-year-old child, anything was better then getting her head chopped off.

"You know, now that I think of it I was always either unbearably hot or icy cold, except when I was free, or maybe I just remember those sad times the most.

"At the Hawkins Plantation, the morning dawned hot and humid. The folks in the cabins stirred their mush wishing they could sit in the noonday shade like some masters did. Dragging their tired bodies out into the yard they stood silently waiting for the overseer to instruct them which field they must work today.

"General Hopkins was always out there sitting on his horse waiting. It was almost as though he were just as much a slave to this parcel of land as the black folks. His father had left this incredibly rich land to him as he was their only child. It had sucked out the life out from his father just as it was sucking the life out of every worker white or black that tilled the land or planted the cotton the land, it demanded to be worked rain or shine, and was a shackle around the General's neck.

"Patrick, the General's overseer was hand picked by the General, he neither beat, nor berated the workers as most overseers did and his workers gave a good days work. The children didn't work as hard as their parents but they were in the fields where the mothers could watch over them and keep them out of trouble.

"All the other fields were planted with cotton, but this one worn out field was being used for raising tobacco. It was a test to see if tobacco would grow in used up fields.

"Ramona's mother had six children, two girls and four boys. Ramona, Jewel, were the oldest then came Henry, John, and the runaway Tatro and of course baby, Jefferson, who was crawling on the blanket that his mama had spread on the ground. Baby goos and gurgles could be heard when the chants of the workers faded.

"Ramona was in the field with her mama but she was looking slanty eyed at Patrick; she didn't want him to notice her watching him. When he took off his hat and wiped the sweat from his face with a piece of red cloth, she bolted for the trees that lined the field. Crouching down in the underbrush she shook with fear as she thought about what would happen if she were caught. She knew that General Hopkins would have no say in her punishment. The Plantation Owners Collective would decide the punishment. Ruthless plantation owners made up the Collective, men who were always losing slaves because of their inhumane treatment, had formed the Collective and its main objective was to find and return runaway slaves. They always dealt out severe punishment to the runaways, but it did little to deter the black fugitives.

"Ramona's Mama who had seen her leave on the west side of the field stood up and began waving her arms and shouting praise to the lord above. She was desperately trying to attract attention away from her child who was bent low and rushing toward the woods.

"Get back to work," Patrick had shouted.

"Her mama bent down to pick another boll of cotton while she prayed, sweet Jesus, protect my lowly child from the wrath of the devil and Master Jessie,"

"The songs of the workers lulled the frightened child; the other workers had seen her escape but they kept right on working and singing. Joyous songs began to ring out as the day wound down to a tired but hopeful night.

"The child's escape had gone unnoticed by the overseer and the black community was filled with elation. One little child had escaped the abuse by a white man. The black compound of workers wordlessly celebrated Ramona's escape and prayed for her safety.

"When morning came the workers filed out of their cabins and waiting for them was General Hopkins and Master Jessie.

"Master Jessie wore an evil grin that sent shivers of fear through the crowd of slaves. The tension was so thick you could almost cut it with a knife.

"It has come to my attention that one of the children is missing." Shouted Master Jessie as he sat angrily on his overly burdened horse.

"We don't want to have to question every one of you to find out what happened to the girl, now do we? My overseer has no problem dealing out the right kind of punishment to the guilty party."

"Sir," said General Hopkins indignantly, "I don't think that any harsh punishment will be necessary, my workers are loyal to me and they will cooperate to the fullest."

"Well, I have my doubts about their loyalty, but I do know that a whip will get the information I need."

"How did you come into the information that one of my people was even missing?" asked the confused General.

"There is a man amongst your workers who will do anything for a jug of corn liquor. He keeps me informed about events on this farm. I'm telling you this so you will be well aware of just how loyal your people really are."

"The workers cast glances around the crowd trying to guess which man had sold out to Master Jessie for a jug of hooch. Their looks landed on Jake a slovenly man who had been bought a few months ago at auction and who was now slyly working his way to the back of the crowd. The other slaves parted away from this traitor and he stood exposed for the beast that he was. From the wicked looks that flashed his way I'm sure that he never again had a chance to betray anyone else."

"Now you understand that this is the story Ramona told me as we hid from the men who were always after us. Much of the story came later from other slaves we met along the trail to freedom."

Jessie's face took on soft glow as she spoke Ramona's name.

"Many a night we talked the night away to keep from crying, meanwhile Ramona, her legs cramping from scrunching under a bush, grew tired of hiding in the brush and had edged her way out of the hot dry branches. *I would give anything for a drink of water*, she thought as she made her way deeper into the forest. Always listening for the sounds of people and dogs, she pushed further into the woods until she could walk no more. She sat down near a scrubby tree that was stunted by the huge poplars that towered above it. *It's just like me drying up from needing water,* she thought as her head nodded and she fought the sleep that was stealing over her. Sleep won and she snuggled down next to the unfortunate little tree and slept. Hours later she woke with a start, *what was that noise?* She heard it again and recognized it as the sound of cows crying for someone to relieve them from their misery. Somebody is gonna come and herd them cows to the barn soon, better get over there and see what they crying about, maybe even get some of the milk that's causing them such misery."

"Throat parched, stomach empty, she made her way came to the stream where the cows were standing in the water. She pushed her way through the herd and she slipped down into the water, floating in the muddy stream she told me that she had never felt more alive.

*"For the first time in my life no one is here to tell me what to do. I'm almost free, all I have to do is find Tatro and we can go north. North is where folks didn't own other folks."* Her fervor made her free.

"Gone was the hunger for food, gone were all thought of milking the cows. Savoring that fleeting taste of freedom had filled her whole being. She yearned for nothing more.

"The feeling of being watched stole over Ramona, she slowly slid up on the bank and cautiously looked around at the woods that were being gobbled up by the night, her eyes searched the hill behind which the sun was retreating.

"She said she saw nothing at first, then she squinted her eyes and saw something in the underbrush, her mind told her it was a child but then she thought, *it can't be,* When she saw me she wondered how I had gotten lost out here in this nowhere.

"Come child." Ramona questioned, "What's yer name and why you out here, you lost or what?"

"My name's Jessie, I runned away," I said as I began to sniffle.

"Jessie, you can't run away, you too small," Ramona told me.

"Well I did, so there," I shouted, "I aint gonna let Master Jessie cut off my head."

"Ain't nobody gonna cut off your head, they don't do that, you worth too much money to them."

" Jack, the overseer tole me so, he say if he take me back from the auction Master Jessie gonna be mad cause he cain't sell me so he gonna cut off my head. I don't want that so I runned."

"Lordy day, why we got so much misery in this here world?" Mourned Ramona. "We gotta get out of here and find food and rest, they gonna be after us soon. One slave missing is bad, two missing is dreadful."

"I hear tell my brother Tatro is hiding in these here woods," Ramona tried to comfort me, "if we find him maybe we be safe."

"First we gonna git some of that milk from these over full cows, stick your head down here so I can aim the teat at your mouth. Good now open and stay still." I never could remember when I had tasted anything so good.

"That's enough can't have you getting sick from too much food at once," cautioned Ramona. "Now it's my turn," she said as she turned the teat toward her own mouth.

"I was the first to hear the dogs and I punched Ramona on the shoulder to get her attention. Ramona listened for a moment then she motioned for me to follow her into the stream. We waded down stream until Ramona thought it would be safe to leave the water. Taking my shaking hand, Ramona rushed me toward the darkening forest.

"Once we were in the security of the nearly dark woods I pulled my hand away from Ramona's grip and announced, "I gotta pee!"

The absurdity of the announcement struck Ramona so funny that she burst out laughing. As I squatted to relieve myself, I watched my new friend suspiciously, *jist what was so funny?*

"We soon found a spot where we could rest and still see the path leading through the woods.

"Can't have somebody sneaking up on us, an that's for sure." Warned Ramona.

"Although the days were blistering hot the nights were often cool and damp, especially in the deep woods. We huddled together for comfort and warmth.

"Ramona later told me she had a hard time getting to sleep that first night because her mind was going lickity split trying to find a answer to her problem and figure what to do with me. What am I doing taking up with this child when I gotta move fast if I don't want to end up Master Jessie's whore, Ramona had silently reasoned. Funny she got the same name as the man I running from."
"Gotta ask her more about where she from and why she running away from her folks. Can't believe they would let her run from the white man when she so small. She sure got a tale about Jack cutting her head off, wonder where she got that. Sleep wiped away all the questions from her mind and she tossed and turned until dawn.

"When she opened her eyes again there I sat staring at her. She jumped up

*JESSIE'S FLIGHT TO FREEDOM*

and asked, "What's wrong Jessie, did I hear something?"

"I'm hungry. I shook you, and shook you, and you wouldn't wake up." I lowered my head and whispered, "I was getting scared."

"Well, yer right to be scared, we gotta get as far away from this place as we can, but first I gotta find my brother. Tatro almost white and he kin pass, maybe he can get us out of here by saying we his slaves. Maybe he take us up north where they ain't no slaves, wouldn't that be something?"

"I don't wanta go north, they ain't nobody I knows there," I sobbed.

"Come on we gotta go find Tatro, and some food."

"I ain't been so hungry in all my life," grumbled Ramona, "sure wish I had some off mama's fried bread, I kin almost smell it."

"I smell it too," I cried out. "It's coming from over that there hill." I started to run toward the lush green knoll, and Ramona had no other choice but to follow.

"When we came to the top of the rise we seen a campfire at the edge of the woods, but we couldn't see anyone. We slowly crept down the hill hiding behind every bush and tree as we made our way toward the fire, where a pan with sizzling bacon sat unattended."

"Don't touch nothing," Ramona warned Jessie, "we get caught stealing we gonna get hung."

"I began to cry, my guts were tearing at me for food and here was food within reach.

"Ramona said she couldn't stand my crying any longer; and grabbing the skillet from the fire she dumped the contents on the grass where the thick slabs of bacon would cool fast."

"Reaching out, I picked up one of the still hot slices and crammed it into my mouth. I greedily chewed the hot meat, grimacing and opening my mouth every other chew to help the cool the blistering food. Ramona said later that she would have laughed at the funny faces I was making if the situation were not so serious.

"Delightedly rubbing my tummy, I swallowed my first morsel of food in the three days that I had been on the run. While reaching for another slice of the succulent meat, I became aware of the white man who was standing in the shadow of tree watching us."

*I ain't gonna give up this bit of bacon, even if he do cut my head off,* I thought.

"You that hungry that you gonna burn your mouth to fill your gut?" Asked the white man.

"Yas Sir." I Answered.

*Don't do no good to whine and snot, he never knowd hungry. Can't even tell him why you hungry, he turns you in, he only know white ways.*

*What that fool Ramona doing hugging that white man? I questioned wordlessly, She one foolish nigra!*

"I kept on chewing my chunk of bacon while I watched my new friend and the white man exchange hugs and kisses.

"Ramona couldn't believe her luck, escaping the dogs and finding Tatro so soon was too good to be real.

"Jessie, this is my brother Tatro, he's been on the run for a long time. We can travel north with him."

"Ramona pulled me foreword and pressed my hand onto Tatro's. "Say howdy do to Tatro."

"Why you white, Ramona ain't?" I asked backing away suspiciously. I don't like to touch a white man's hand. They do bad things with their hands"

"I know Jessie, but when we get to the North all that will be over, Northern men don't hurt little girls," Ramona prayed that what she told the child about northern men was true.

"Why you running, child ain't you got folks to care for you? Don't hardly make any sense, a child on the run. Who is you Papa?"

I stood straight and tall as my small frame would allow and answered, "Master Jessie Jonas is my Papa, he say I too black to be his child. My mama named me after him. He wants to sell me, but nobody buys."

"I running from Master Jessie too," exclaimed Ramona. "He want me for bad reasons."

"Oh sheet, another mixed bastard like me! Ain't your fault child." Tatro knelt down and cupped my small face with both of his work roughened hands and gently asked, "Where you mama?"

"She died when I was borned," I answered calmly.

"We gonna have to move real soon, we pressing our luck even having a fire going out here in the open. I was hoping the smell of food would guide you to me little sister, but I never expected you to bring a child with you."

"We gonna eat the rest of this food ain't we," I whispered.

"We sure are," answered Tatro.

"Throwing chunks of brown dough into the sizzling grease, Tatro sat back and smiled at the girls.

"Now we living," he said as the bread began to bubble and rise.

"When the fry bread was cool enough to handle we finished off both the side pork and bread.

"Yawning and fighting sleep, I was the first to feel exhaustion creeping in on my tired little body. The stress of the chase had sapped all of our strength.

"Bellies full we all got real drowsy, heads drooped, eyes fluttered, and we soon were asleep.

"Startled awake by a sound that she didn't recognize, Ramona jumped up and frantically searched the woods in which they were hiding.

"Her frantic behavior woke Tatro and me.

"What is it, what woke you, did you hear something? Questioned Tatro.

"I heard a loud crashing off yonder," answered Ramona anxiously, "I thought it was the gang of white men hunting for us."

"That's probably just a tree falling in the woods. I've heard a lot of trees crashing in the last couple of weeks. This woods is old and trees die just like folks die. Sides the white man don't make noise when he creeping up on you, they're sneaky.

"Little sister, It be getting full dark soon, if we start now and travel at night," encouraged Tatro, "we just might reach north in a couple of days."

"Sitting on the ground next to me, Ramona tried to reassure the me by telling me that we were gonna make it, we were gonna get away from those folks that hate us and make a new life."

"Little sister," Tatro whispered quietly, "they ain't no place that some folks don't hate us, we black and they white, that's the difference and that difference is why they hate us."

"Tatro you look white so white folks don't hate you."

"Tatro stood and began pacing back and forth rubbing his head; after a few moments he hunkered down close to the fire and told us, that he may be white on the outside but he was black on the inside. That's hard to forget when I'm with the white folks, it's as though they can see right through me. I'm not sure I can pass, and I'm scared as hell they gonna hang my ass for trying to act white."

"You sure look white to me, I was scared we was caught when I first seen you," I confirmed.

"Well, we sure gonna try," bragged Tatro, "all they can do is bring us back, ain't that so little sister?

"You gonna be our good luck," Tatro whispered as he patted my head. "Little Jessie, we gonna be north before you know it!"

"Tatro began packing up the few articles that he had backpacked when he first took off on the run; Tatro regretted leaving his sanctuary in the woods. Suddenly he paused in his packing to listen, *was that the sound of an animal or a man creeping through the woods? Best not scare the girls; if we hurry we can git away before we finds out.*

"Frantically searching the edge of the trees and pretending he was angry, he snarled, come on ladies, I ain't got all day?"

"Eyes wild, his voice rich with fear, Tatro suddenly shouted, run and run we did!"

"Men on horseback rolled in like an all-consuming wave, guns drawn, faces filled with hate. Surrounding the terrified Tatro, they circled him all the while whipping at his face and shouting obscenities.

"Tatro danced away from the whips whenever he could praying that he could keep the men busy while the girls got away. *They will stop soon. I can stand this whipping. I can take whatever they hand out if the girls are safe.*

"They had the man they wanted, Tatro had run and stayed free for almost a month. They couldn't have that.

"We got to teach them a lesson they won't forget," shouted one of the posses. "If this black bastard gets away with running, soon all the nigger's will be running and we won't have any black to work the land. Got to hang that bastard, show those other niggers that it don't pay to run."

"When we could run no further, we dropped down to the sun-scorched grass. Shaking with fear and anger Ramona beat the ground where she lay.

"Why'd you do that?" I questioned.

"Cause them no good whities caught my brother, and I don't know what they gonna do to him."

"Maybe they gonna cut off his head," I offered.

"Don't you say that, he's my brother," hissed Ramona, then she gently added, "We need him to help us git north."

"Terrible screams invaded the meadow where we had fallen; Tatro's hoarse voice was filled with unbearable agony.

"In the distance we could hear the men laughing and shouting, more screams, then deadly silence."

"Nodding my head in affirmation, I announced that they had cut off his head just like I said."

"Oh God in heaven, please save Tatro," begged Ramona.

"After waiting what seemed like days, we crept back to the place where we had left Tatro. The dawn was flooding over the horrific scene as we came over the rise and surveyed the open patch at the edge of the woods.

"Tatro was still there, hanging from the tree, his trousers torn from his body and thrown into a branch beside him. Tatro's bare feet hung lifelessly pointing down toward the blood-spattered earth below, while his mutilated face sagged against the rope that suspended him. The body of Tatro had been whipped repeatedly and then castrated. This was supreme insult to a gentle man who only wanted to be free.

'Them dirty bastards, they killed my brother," whispered Ramona.

"They didn't cut his head off," I offered.

"Goddamn it, he just as dead!" agonized Ramona. "looky what they done to his manhood. Weeping copiously, she commanded me, "Remember this! This is what the white man does to black folk."

"As a seven-year-old child I didn't realize the meaning of the castration, but I did realize that Tatro was dead and our chances of reaching safety were in danger.

"Can't even bury him, gotta leave him hanging like a scarecrow in the wind." Ramona's bitterness was so tangible that it was as if it were a weight pulling her down into hell.

"We better git outta here," I pleaded, "those bad men might come back."

"Ramona grabbed what was left of Tatro's knapsack, after the horses had trampled it. Tightly hugging the canvas bag to her breast as though a part of Tatro was still in the knapsack, she whispered, *it's all I have left of my beloved Tatro.*

"Bare feet twisting, finger wrapping the front of my tattered dress, I stood watching my friend suffer from the loss of her brother. My heart was pounding, I needed to run, but I couldn't leave Ramona.

"The far away sound of a tree crashing in the woods stirred Ramona, grabbing my hand she whispered, "Come on!"

"It was just a tree falling, but we didn't know that.

"As we ran we tried to keep the sun over their right shoulder, for that is what Tatro had said he was going to do before he lit out for the north.

"The pace slowed after we had run about a mile, trying to catch our breath we crawled into some underbrush and huddled there gasping. We spent the day hiding waiting for the darkness to conceal us from the hunters.

"Night was filled with strange sounds, and our imaginations were running full tilt. The darkest parts of the night made me feel the safest. Thrashing through the woods we often stumbled over dead trees, mounds of earth and piles of debris that had settled onto the earth. We had nothing but the moon to guide us and it was often covered by clouds. Dawn found us foraging for food; we both were beyond caring if animals were about. Our need for food was greater than our fear of the unknown.

"The sound of a stream gurgling filtered into our conscience and the melody of the brook drew our parched bodies to the welcoming sound. Looking around for any hidden enemy at first we failed to notice the beauty of our hiding place. We later decided that this meadow, with a cold running stream, framed by woods was a picture perfect place to rest and plan. Would we be safe here, time would tell. Fear tore at our guts but thirst and hunger overwhelmed it. Here we were, two young healthy females eating so little that our bodies were close to consuming themselves.

"Having slaked our thirst, we lay in the brush and rested. Dreams of food began to invade my every thought. I was so weak that my eyes kept closing for sleep, but my growling stomach would wake me. Ramona sat leaning against a hearty shrub and staring in the direction that she thought was north, wondering if they would ever make it.

"Seeing the black man riding across the meadow on a horse didn't register with Ramona's weary brain. When the realization that it was a real person finally penetrated her mind, Ramona put her fingers to her lips and shushed my groaning. I reached out and grabbed Ramona's hand and together we watched as the man drew closer to the brush where we lay hiding.

# Chapter Four

We must be North," whispered Ramona, "I ain't never seen a black man ride a horse before!"

I only nodded; I was too frightened to say anything. I had wet myself again. The shame I felt as I lay on my stomach and felt the urine soaking through the front of my tattered dress prevented me from feeling any happiness.

"Should we ask him, I'm scared to try and scared not to." Ramona made the decision and sat up, pushed herself out of the wild shrub, and brushing the dust off, shouted to the rider.

"I followed her lead.

"What you two doing out here in the nowhere?" asked the handsome black man, all the while staring at Ramona with puzzled eyes.

"We north yet?" demanded Ramona.

"No girl, you ain't north, is that where your heading?"

"Yes sir," I piped up, "we gonna be free an I gonna be Ramona's little sister."

"That your name?" He asked, looking at the older girl.

"Yes sir, an this here's Jessie, we headed north."

"You on the run?" The man asked.

"We just headed north!" insisted the older girl.

"That your child?" Asked the curious black man.

"We just headed north," Ramona evaded the question determinedly."

"Well, Ramona we just headed north, you and your little sister are welcome to stay at my place for as long as you need."

"You must be some rich nigger, riding a horse, and have a place to take folks."

"Well, little Jessie, I ain't rich, but I ain't poor. I always have a place for folks on the run."

Ramona stared right into the mans face and insisted, "I ain't never said we on the run, don't you forget that."

"Come on my place is just about a mile down the road. You will get food and rest for as long as you need it."

"If you think we runaways why you take us in?" demanded Ramona

"You look like you need help and my offer still stands, take it or leave it."

"We take it for now," answered Ramona suspiciously.

"Well, it's about time you used some sense. My name is David, and you can call me Mr. David. Just what is that child to you, is she yours?"

"As we walked along side the horse we pretended to answer the questions Mr. David asked.

"She belongs to me, she my little sister." Mama always told Ramona that God didn't count lies if you crossed your fingers, so that is what she did when she answered Mr. David with her lie.

"Well, if you say so," replied Mr. David, "but she don't even look like you. She real black."

"Why you always say well?" I asked, "it sound funny, like you talking bout water."

"Well, I don't know, guess I didn't even know when I say it. Most likely learned it from the white folks I lived with."

"You lived with white folks. Did they beat you?" I persisted. Looking up at the man on horseback, I failed to see the cow paddy lying in the path and stepped right in it.

"I done stepped in shit, Ramona," I cried, "I stepped right in it, I gonna die now for sure."

"No you ain't," Ramona assured me, "you gonna be alright as soon as I wash the stuff off, now stop that bellering."

"Looky there Jessie, that's Mr. David's house, ain't it grand?............Jessie, never mind that mess just look where we gonna stay."

"Meanwhile I was preoccupied with scrubbing my filthy foot with grass that I had torn from the lush green lawn, that I didn't even glance in that direction. When I did finally look to where Ramona was pointing, I stared in awe, "How you get that big house?" I asked suspiciously.

"Well, the white folks that I lived with gave me this piece of land when their son died, it was supposed to go to him and they didn't have anybody else to give it to. They said I was just like a son to them and I jumped at the chance to have my own place. The house wasn't here when I first took over but with hard work and the help of my nigras I was able to build it a few years ago."

*JESSIE'S FLIGHT TO FREEDOM*

"You got black folks working for you?" I demanded.

David reluctantly nodded his head.

"You still friends with those white folks?" asked Ramona.

"Well, of course I am, they are my protection. There's men out there that want to hang every free nigra they see. I have a pact with those folks, I don't cause trouble for them and they leave me alone."

"You were a slave?" asked the confused Ramona.

"Well, I didn't know I was a slave for a long time, the white folks treated me good, like their own son. When I wanted to leave they told me that I was their property, ain't never been property before. It cut my heart out to be slave to the family I loved."

"We had reached the path in front yard of the big house just as the down stairs maid, came out the front door.

"Nance, you see to it that these folks are fed and meanwhile Ramona, you and little sister can find a cabin in the back of the house that is empty and stay as long as you want."

"I completely forgot about the dung on my right heel as I stared up at the great white house that Mr. David had built. The white washed boards gleamed in sun-drenched afternoon searing a yearning into my empty soul. *Oh God, to have a safe place like this to call home. That would be heaven.*

"Mr. David must have recognized the look in the my eyes and thought, *Well, now I know what will work in keeping these two here, at least for a while.*

The cabin was plain, wood floors, bare of any furnishings except two racks built on the far wall.

"Somebody live here once," remarked Ramona.

"Now it be ours, we lucky," confirmed Jessie.

"Gotta get some hay for sleeping, but first let's git some food from that Nance girl."

"Yes mam," I agreed with delight, the thought of sitting down and eating food without being on the lookout for white gangs of men chasing us, caused me to feel faint. As we headed back toward the house Ramona reminded me, "Jessie, we gotta watch what we say in front of these folks, don't really know em. We just can't trust anybody."

"When we reached the low built stoop at the back of the house, Nance was waiting for us with bowls of potatoes soup and a plate heaped with wedges of corn bread. We were weak from hunger, but we only stared at the feast that was awaiting us. Ramona touched the still warm corn bread and when no whip sting came on our back, we dug in."

"Mr. David sat in his study and day dreamed the rest of his plan for the future. *If it's one thing the white folks taught me it is how to get what you want and not worry about how many people you have to walk over to get it. That gal Ramona is perfect for me; she will make a fine-looking mistress for this place,* thought Mr. David; *we would have many handsome sons. I can see it all now. She should be more than happy to stay where she is safe, all I have to do is get rid of that child she's dragging around with her. When Ramona is settled in I will see to it the child disappears.*

"Squatting on the low built back stoop of the great house, we finished eating potato soup and all the corn bread. Returning the now empty bowls and plate to Nance, we again thanked her for all the vittles that had filled our gut. Tummies full, the heat of the sun, the wafting of an occasional cool breeze and with the shrinking of fear, weariness stole over us causing us to yawn and stretch out under the closest tree. This is where Mr. David found us hours later.

"Seems all we do lately is sleep," complained Ramona as she groaned and rolled over toward me who had just wakened. "Mr. David gonna think we lazy no account nigras."

"We tired from running, thas all," I explained.

"Sit up and look perky, here he comes now." Ramona jumped to her feet and helped me up. We stood at attention waiting for Mr. David to come closer.

"Ramona was all too aware of her shabby dress and filthy bare feet as she waited for our rescuer to approach. What she didn't realize is that the sunlight behind her outlined her lush young body through her tattered dress.

*"My God she's beautiful,* thought Mr. David, as he approached the waiting nomads. *I will have her,* he promised himself.

"Nance watched the episode from the back door. She had noticed the way the master behaved around the new girl and delighted in the fact that his interest in her was waning. Mr. David was used to getting what he wanted and the new girl is what he wanted. Living with white folks had done that to him, turned him into a White Nigger. *Should I warn her,* she questioned her conscience, *no, the unlucky girl will have to find out for herself.*

"I immediately noticed Mr. David's lecherous inspection of Ramona, *Why he looking so funny at Ramona. He scaring me with his smiling ways.*

"Ramona, shifting one foot in front of the other, smiled at her champion creating a tempting picture for the now enthralled Master David.

"Well now, you're wise in resting here under this old tree instead of in those hot cabins, not a breath of air gets in there on these hot days. I've decided you can work in my house instead of the fields, if that meets with your satisfaction.

Can't have such delicate young girls picking cotton, that's for the common nigra."

"You Ramona will sleep in the main house and Nance will assign you your duties, the child will work in the kitchen, Sophia will see to her. Now it is about time we got you settled into the house don't you think?"

"Master David I don't want to be contrary but I need to be near my little sister at night. Will it be alright if I sleep in the cabin with her?"

"Master wasn't happy about that idea but he pretended it wasn't important and told her to sleep where she wished."

"The weeks flew as we two runaways settled into the household routine, Ramona cleaned the upstairs bedrooms and did the laundry, I helped Sophia prepare the meals for the Master and his guests.

"Sophia took extra care to see that I had enough food and that my duties were light enough for a seven year old. The Master had given me a new dress, it was a bit large, but Sophia teased, "If you keep on eating like that you will grow into it."

"Me and Ramona still slept in the same cabin, but seen less and less of each other during the day. I was angry with Master and I said so to Sophia.

"He always has some reason why Ramona gotta work late or help him entertain his highfalutin guests."

"Don't you be saying that around anybody else, you hear? Them is dangerous words. Folks gotta watch what they say round here."

"What you mean," I asked.

"I said what I said and I ain't gonna say no more." Sophia continued beating the batter for corn bread; her eyes had a far away look, she had escaped to another realm that even I couldn't enter.

Weeks grew into months and still the Master kept Ramona busy entertaining his friends. To me, it was almost as though Ramona were in training to become mistress of the house. But that couldn't be, owners didn't marry slaves and slaves are what we are.

I had developed a great dislike for the Master. Him and his sneaky ways, always pretending he likes me when I see hate in his eyes when Ramona ain't looking. I don't trust him, he up to something and when I figure it out, we gone.

Ramona who was taken in by Master David's generosity couldn't get over the fact that she was being treated like she really mattered.

"Jessie, life is getting better and better for us on Master David's place. He protects us from the white folks and treats us good, that's all we can ask. I ain't never been treated so good in all of my twelve years, wait,......It

July.........now I is thirteen, my birthday was last week in June and I jest forgot. I getting grown up and I don't have to fear nothing from Mr. Jessie Jones."

"Something wrong here, I still want to go north, maybe it bes better there too." I tried to explain my fears to Ramona but my vocabulary wasn't adequate enough to contain the words betrayer, coward, liar, and false-hearted.

"You know little Jessie, you getting older too, time you got to wearing drawers under that dress, you know how men are when they see a bare bottom." Ramona giggled as she strutted around the shack and shook her petite little bottom at me.

"The very next day when Ramona came back from Master David's house she had a pair of white cotton drawers in her hand. "Here you go, your first pair of grown up drawers and I even sewed your name in them."

"I felt both proud and uncomfortable wearing my first pair of cotton under drawers that my friend Ramona had made for me. No more peeing where I stand, I vowed. *If I'm getting growed up why do I feel so scared all the time?* My heart questioned."

"Another landmark had passed for me without the security and guidance of a mother and father. Something was missing, the emptiness was crowding my gut, I didn't know what it was but I had to keep on searching for that precious something to fill the void.

"While we were preparing the noonday meal, Nance suddenly burst out crying and me and Sophie could only stand and watch frightened, as Nance frantically beat her stomach and breast. When she had spent all of her fury, she collapsed into a chair and sobbed brokenheartedly.

"Why you pound yourself like that," I had asked.

"Cause, Jessie, I'm gonna have that bastard chile of Mr. David's and I don't want it. I gotta fornicate with him, but I don't have to like it."

"What's fornicate mean, is that how you get babies? I asked. Is that the way my mama got me, fornicating, is he gonna fornicate us too?"

"Never you mind what fornicating mean," Sophie warned, "you'll find out soon enough."

"Oh chile," Nance lamented, "I don't know, all I do know is I ain't having this chile, I'll die first............. We sooo lucky to be women, man want us, man gets us and we have no say! You wait, you gonna get your turn too."

"Why you can't say no to Mr. David?"

"Cause little Jessie, he give me to the white folks, say I'm a runaway and they beat me, maybe kill me."

"But ain't he Negro like us, why he act white?"

"Cause he half white and he raised with white folks and that makes him white as them. He a bastard thas all, he don't want me or this chile he just want my comfort in his bed. Now he up to working on Miss Ramona, she his next comfort."

"Nance spit on the fish she had prepared for Mr. David's lunch, wiped the sweat from under her arms on the sweet potatoes that she placed next to the fish, nodded her head in agreement with some unseen source and took the plate into the dinning room for the waiting Mr. David.

"I watched with worry, *if Nance is treated this way by Mr. David what he gonna do to us, he gonna fornicate us too?*

"Mr. David had his own plan simmering. First he gotta get rid of Miss Fancy Nance and that kid she's carrying, it gonna be dark for sure. She too dark skinned for it not to be. Now that Miss Ramona, she's some tasty dish, bet she got some mighty sweet sugar between her legs, and she light skinned too, I would have handsome sons from that union, might even have to marry this one.

"Sophie the old black women that had cooked for Mr. David since he moved into his own home had developed a liking for me. She was bound and determined to teach me everything she knew about cooking all the scrumptious meals that Mr. David insisted he be served. I listened close while Sophie explained the reason why she par-boiled the ham first or why she added a touch of milk to the scrambled eggs. She taught me to strain the goats milk and make cottage cheese. Sophie called it, Clouds From Heaven, so that is what I called it too.

"One morning when I was rushing around wiping the unending red dust off cupboards, tables and windowsills, Sophia warned me to slow down she said us niggers supposed to move slow. Fast moving niggers scare white folks."

"My days were filled with learning everything that Sophie could teach me and my nights were filled with the fear that Mr. David was going to steal Ramona away.

"I pretended that I didn't hear the whispers from the two women while they worked in the kitchen, but my ears were tuned to the very tremor of Sophie's voice. The more I heard the more I worried and Ramona wouldn't believe my warnings.

"Ramona couldn't figure out why Nance had gone back to working in the fields. She seemed so happy to be away from the house and Master David. She was big with child but still she worked in the fields with the other black folks and she smiled constantly while she labored.

"It all came to a head the day the Plantation Owners Collective, came to challenge Mr. David. They demanded he show papers for all his slaves.

"We been hearing rumors about you taking in runaways and hiding them here." Shouted Ned Horton, the self appointed leader of the group.

"Mr. David invited them and his overseer, Big Fred, into his office and showed him the papers for twenty slaves that were presently working on his plantation.

"We been watching and you got more than this many blackies working here." Ned could neither read nor write so he dismissed the papers as if they were not worth worrying about.

"Well, I could bring them all in from the fields for you to count, but it would mean I would lose a days labor from them. Someone would have to make up for the money I might lose that day. Are any of you ready to put forth your money to replace my loss? "Asked Mr. David.

"Ned Horton was in no position to replace anyone's lost wages, his shack was near to falling down and the wife and six children kept him struggling to keep food on the table. His only source of pride was the leadership status he maintained with the Plantation Owners Collective.

"Don't you get uppity with me you black son-of-a-bitch, I don't take back talk from no white nigger. You watch yer self when yer speaking to me, you hear? My place in life might be low on the totem pole, but you goddamn niggers are lower and I'm gonna let you know it.

"Mr. David, my ass you're a nigger too, just a little whiter then most. I gotta keep my eyes on you; you're too slick for my liking. We gonna keep checking on you an you better not have any unpapered darkies around when we come again" Ned warned Mr. David.

"The whole plantation had known from the first horse's breath as they rode up to the house, that trouble was coming soon.

"Me and Ramona had hidden in the kitchen; we lay flat under the floorboards of the wood box. The wood box covered one wall and had been built for just that purpose, to hide runaways. We found out later that Mr. David didn't believe in buying slaves, he believed in confiscating them and holding them by fear and intimidation.

"When the coast was clear, Mr. David called Big Fred, and all the house blacks together and announced, "There ain't nobody to leave this place less I signs for you, no sneaking out for meetings, no fornicating, no nothing. I don't want that white trash to be able to count you or catch you off my land. You all know who I got papers on so watch your step."

"Ramona," I begged, "we gotta get out of here, there's gonna be trouble, Sophia says the white farmers are tired of a nigger like Mr. David, acting high and mighty over them and they gonna make him pay."

"Mr. David got too many white acquaintances, they won't let anything happen to their friend. Jessie, I'm getting sick and tired of hearing how we should leave the only place where we safe, please stop nagging me about it." Ramona pleaded.

Sophia fretted, "Mr. David's pretty upset over those men coming to his house las week and acting like he a criminal, somebody gonna pay and it won't be Nance, she laid up with losing that baby she didn't want no how."

"Sophia, who else is there to pay" I innocently asked.

"Why, child figure it out yourself, it be your friend Ramona. Mr. David, he been sniffing round after her ever since you come here."

"No," I shouted. "He not gonna get her, he fornicates with Nance, not Ramona. We on our way north, we can't stay here."

"Mr. David get anything he want, oh, he just as spiteful as white folks," stated Sophia. "If he don't get what he want he gonna put her in the sling."

"Big eyed, I asked, "What's the sling?

"It a rope seat that hangs in the tree in the front of the house, you tied in there till you give in and do what the master wants, no food, no water, you pee and crap on yourself, and those damn dogs circle waiting for you to die. He don't feed the dogs either, so they mighty hungry. I ain't seen nobody that didn't give in."

"I didn't believe Sophia's story, but the thought of anyone being tied in the sling scared the anger out of me. I didn't argue anymore with the cantankerous Sophia, but I made up my mind that I would spoil Mr. David's wicked plans for Ramona.

"I started that very night with a small lie. While get ready for bed I off handily stated, "Mr. David say I should fix my hair in a different way. He say it show my pretty face."

"Why he say that," Ramona questioned. "Did he say anything about me?"

"No, he didn't say nothing bout you, just me," I answered the smiling.

"That strange since he pursue me all the time, I can't hardly hold him off most times."

"Maybe he tired of pursuing you and he sniffing round somebody else."

"Well, we both too young for what he have in mind, maybe we better hit out for the North when this trouble settles."

"*Thank you God,*" I thought.

# Chapter Five

Heart singing, I went to my mat on the floor of the cabin and huddled down ready for sleep. It had been a long day and I was exhausted. "The sun was barely up when the men came crashing into the room with guns pointing at us cowering on our mats.

"We had automatically jumped together when the terrible noise tore us from our sleep. People were lined up in the front of the slave cabins, some were crying but most were standing resolutely waiting for whatever the white man had in mind.

"Mr. David's arm was being twisted behind his back by one of the raiders and he looked frightened. Big Fred stood off to one side not saying or doing anything.

"We're looking for a slave women about fifteen and we heard she's here, so all you women line up and show your teeth so we can see how old you are. You old women don't need to come foreword, we can see for ourselves when you're too old!"

"Give us the girl and we let the rest of you go," shouted one of the men in the Plantation Owners Collective posse.

"Must be some important black bitch for Mr. Jessie Jonas to put out a reward for her capture," commented one of the raiders.

"Ain't ya ever seen his wife?" Asked a gray haired, craggy faced fellow with brown eyes and teeth to match. " That old women of his would gag a maggot off a gut wagon. If I was married to that I'd be looking for a sweet piece of tail too, course I wouldn't be paying such a high price for that tail."

"Ramona stood out amongst the work worn women like a beacon in a storm. I clung to her hoping that they would think I was Ramona's daughter, but it didn't work. Ramona's slim hips and slender body gave her away. It was obvious she had never given birth."

"Here's the one were looking for," shouted Ned Horton, "your name Ramona?"

"Yes sir, but I didn't do anything wrong. I working for Mr. David and minding my own business."

"We taking this here gal and turning her in for the reward, you got anything to say Mr. David, or whatever your bastard name is. You hear this?"

Yes sir. I understand sir," answered the humiliated black man.

"No sir," whined Mr. David, "I don't have any hold on that women. I can't keep track of all the black folks on my land. You know I can't read nor count sir, it's not allowed."

"One of the men in posse tied Ramona's hands and feet together and threw her over the saddle of a horse. Reaching under her skirt he rudely touched Ramona all the while glaring around the crowd and daring any man to object.

"You lucky there's a reward for you," Ned Horton said with a fierce look, "or you'd be running behind this horse all the way back to town."

"I stood frozen, my heart was thudding so hard in my chest that I just knew the men could hear it. What am I gonna do without Ramona, I can't go north without her and I can't go back with her. What gonna happen to her when Mr. Jessie get hold of her?

"The women of the plantation slowly, imperceptibly, almost as a single thought, moved closer to me and surrounded me, so I was partially hidden from the posse.

"As the posse rode off Ned warned Mr. David, that they were going to get their money, and that they would be coming back in a couple of days to check and see if there were any more new faces on this land.

"Those white bastards had ruined his plan, but he had plenty of black folks on which to take revenge. He would erase the contempt he saw in their eyes when he had bowed before that band of white trash. How dare they treat him that way, after all wasn't he two steps higher then them, being a landowner and Master to his slaves should count for something. When he had silently vented his shame and frustrations, he took a deep breath and the fury showed in his bronze face.

"Get back to work! You'll just have to work through the night to make up for time lost, no one will eat or sleep until the west field is picked, bagged, and weighed."

"Ramona felt her stomach churn as the men took her back along a familiar path, "Dear God please don't let them take me back to Mr. Jessie Jonas, he gonna kill me for running." Her prayers were in vain; the journey from the Jonas Plantation that had taken her and Jessie days to reach, had taken only hours to return on horse back.

"The posse had laughed and shouted for the first few miles but as the liquor ran out and the sun got hotter they limited their frivolity to a guffaw once in a while. Every so often one of the men would hit Ramona's upturned butt with his hand or a whip and they would all cheer and egg the each other on, it became a game to see who could hit the hardest.

"Ramona, hanging upside down over the saddle of the horse had no choice but to endure the torture. Don't damage the merchandise," Ned hollered back to the last man who had delivered a painful blow, "Master Jessie Jonas is paying a high price for that black ass." This outrageous part of the story we found out later, after the harm had been done."

Jessie's brokenhearted sobbing filled the room.

"Lorie, I swear to God if I could have killed those bastard I would have without one minute of regret."

"Master David was livid with shame, but he had only done what he had to do. His excuse to himself was that the more black men who owned slaves, the safer the slaves were. It wasn't his fault that they were born slaves and remained slaves, besides he was forced to behave like a white man to exist in this white man's world to protect his property. Feeling right and at peace by his internal debate, he went looking for Nance.

"When Master David had thrown Nance out of his house and bed she, had united with Henry Flatfeet, he being the end product of a union between a black man and a Indian wife. Henry was a soft-spoken man who had been captured by a group of men and sold to a neighbor of Master David. The neighbor soon grew tired of Henry's preaching freedom and took the only thing from him that could hurt and quiet the slave; he sold Henry's woman and twin girls to a tobacco farmer in the next county. Henry had been alone ever since.

"Master David's plantation was the only place that Henry could feel safe. He was a good christen man who led the prayer service whenever the people could gather. Working from first light to darkness left no time for thoughts of organized religion. Their worship of God could be heard throughout the day; songs of devotion, repentance, or release were often heard as they labored.

"Master David frowned on religious services and worked his slaves so hard they had little time or energy for meetings in the dead of night.

"Henry Flatfeet had vowed that no one would ever rip his woman or their children from him again. He simply would never become attached to another woman. His was a constant struggled to live his life, as God would want him to live, this resolve had caused him to reject the favors of any woman after Bertha and the girls were sold. He let the smiling face of Nance meet with stern

*JESSIE'S FLIGHT TO FREEDOM*

rebuffs, but she did not give up her pursuit of, Mr. Preacher Man, a name she had given him.

"When she had become big with child, Henry thought his troubles were over, she was the Master's whore and that was that.

"The day we came to Master David's plantation, Henry knew that trouble was brewing. Praying to God had always been automatic for him, first thing in the morning and last thing at night, but now he found himself praying all day long. "Lord what more trials and tribulations you got for this lowly servant? I try to follow your lead but it so hard, just direct me to your way, and free this servant from the grief and pain of this world. I ain't got but two things in my heart Lord, love and trust, Amen."

"Master David didn't say anything to the rest of the servants but he had Sophia gather up Nance's few belongings and he had them placed on the back step. Nance had seen this happen to other favorites of Master David and she was delighted by the dismissal.

"Her last encounter with him had scared her, his squeezing her neck during the act had almost made her lose her breath, and she was blacking out when he had turned her loose. When her vision had cleared all she could see was his smiling face. Picking up her meager belongings, Nance wandered the compound trying to decide where to put her head down until morning. Her mind told her to go to the one who made her heart sing and she went to Henry's cabin in the dark of night, lying down on the floor next to him she cried out in thanksgiving. "Master David let me go, now I just me, not his whore, not a slave to his hurting. Let me stay here till the child is born, if you don't want me after that I will leave."

"Henry prayed for guidance, here was the women he had eyes for, she had come to him willingly. Her loving presence soothed his soul; he needed this woman to confirm his existence.

"Yes, you can stay for a while, but we not gonna be together. The lord sent you to me but the devil say join with you, and I won't do that till I feel it right."

"Nance didn't say a word just snuggled closer and went to sleep.

"Dawn burst in on the sleeping couple, Nance with her back to Henry while he cradled her with his arms wrapped lightly around her. His hands gently holding her swollen stomach, as if he were holding the child."

"Now you understand this whole episode had taken place one week before the Plantation Owners Collective, and one miserable beast of a man named Ned Horton had come to harass the people at Mr. David's plantation. The fatal day had begun just like any other day in the nigger compound.

"Gotta get to work, sun's up and Master David don't like it when we late." Henry helped Nance to her feet and brushing his hair with his hands said, "I'll fill the basin with clean water so's you can wash the sleep away, can't waste time, the boss passing out the vitals for the day and we gotta get some food for us and that child, can't work on a empty stomach. Maybe I can get a fish for later, I think it be Saturday and we only gots to work till noon."

"While you fishing I can collect some greens to go with it," Nance's radiant face told the whole story, "we gonna have a celebration."

"After collecting their bread and cornmeal from Big Fred, and having stashed it in the cabin, they had headed out to the field hand in hand. Both had been looking foreword to an easy afternoon. When they separated at the bend in the path Henry gave Nance's hand an extra squeeze and whispered, "Till noon my sweet."

"Nance had known her time was near but she had worked just as hard trying to keep up with the rest of the women. When the sharp pains tore through her body and she had dropped to the ground screaming. The workers heard and seen her drop, but they had kept on working. Bodies bent in labor, hearts filled with anguish, toiling over another man's cotton, they had accepted her misery as their own. After all, for human beings who were crushed down every day by another human being and immorally bought and traded as animals, it wasn't that unusual for women to give birth in the field, take care of the child and go back to work.

"The child had slipped into this world with a gush of blood. The stricken Nance held the child but for a moment. Her mind spinning she thought,

*My son is so small, deep sympathy welled into her heart. Dear God, I wish I could love this child. Her thoughts were filled with bitterness. Why did my child have to be born this way?"*

"Using a flat rock for an anvil she laid the umbilical cord on it and hacked at it with a smaller stone. Tying off the end had proved to be a challenge for her weak and shaking hands. The cord had kept slipping from the blood and she wasn't real sure what she was supposed to do with it anyway. Sure she had heard stories from the others, but she had thought one of them would be with her when she was ready. From deep inside her had come an infinite sadness and the fleeting thought, I'm always alone.

"The boy child's gaze had searched for his mother, found her, gave one soft cry of relief and was heard no more.

"Tears blending with the sweat streaming down her face had blurred her vision as she dug a shallow hole using work worn hands; she gently laid her first born in the rich red earth at the edge of the field. Reaching out, with trembling hands, Nance had plucked white cotton from the plant growing closest in the field. Covering her son's grave with the fresh picked cotton, she had prayed. "Dear lord take this child and give him the love and care his mama can't".

"The noon-day sun had beat down, washing the workers with sweat and the age-old fatigue of despair. While they worked, their furtive glances took in the abortive birth, the death and Nance's weak and desperate struggle to bury the child. They hadn't dared help her, for that would take time away from working the fields and their Master didn't allow that. The women had watched through eyes slit with hate, hate for the master, hate for the injustice, and hate for futility of their plight.

"Signaling that it was quitting time, Big Fred had ridden his horse over to Nance, reaching down had hauled her fragile body up onto the animal. In a slow and measured gait he had delivered her to Henry Flatfeet's cabin. Henry took Nance into his cool dark cabin and crying to the good Lord for strength, he tended to the ill-treated girl as best he could.

"They stole Ramona, them bastards stole her and we gotta get her back." I swore vengeance and mayhem on anybody who was holding my friend.

"I'm going to find her and we gonna go north. Thats where we was heading when that fool Master David done waylaid us," I complained with as much derision as a child could muster.

"Sophie, who had grown tired of listening to me grumble, secretly wished that I would indeed find and rescue my friend Ramona; besides, she hated Master David with a passion for his cruelty. She mumbled to Ermine, "He weren't no better then the white men. He uses them for breeding mares and then abandons both them and the children that were born.

"Jessie, go get me a fresh pail of water and be quick about it, I got peas to cook for supper."

"Sophia watched as I grabbed the half empty water pail and she had seen the questioning look pass over my face. Why would she send me for water when the pail was still half full? I decided to sneak back and listen to them and see what they were up to.

"She too smart for her britches," Sophia commented to her friend Ermine.

"Now, if only I can get that new fellow, George to help," Sophia whispered to Ermine, "we stand a chance of getting little Jessie away from here and maybe even on the trail to the north."

"You trust that new fellow, he pretty friendly with Master David," Ermine asked.

"He just sucking up so the Master won't give him up to the posse. I heard him say when things settle down, he gone again; an I want our little Jessie to go with him." Shaking her head dejectedly Sophia murmured, "She never gonna stand a chance here."

"That Mr. David shur got mean since them fellows from the collective came around. Sophia, I wouldn't put it pass him to turn in all the unpapered black folks here abouts, course then he wouldn't have so many to work his land."

"You right Ermine, his first care is for his land, nobody and nothing else count. He wants to be the first rich white nigger, even ifen it come over somebody else's sweat an blood."

"Sh, here he come now and he wearing that look agin, somebody's ass is gonna be in the sling."

" Sophia," he shouted, "where in hell is Miss Fancy Nance, why in hell ain't she in here fixing my dinner?"

"Why Master David you put her out a while back, and now she laid up, didn't she have that chile last week and it being born dead and all? She still grieving I expect."

" She's grieved long enough," Master David snarled, "I need her in here now."

"Yes sir," Sophia answered, all the while thinking, *I just bet you do!*

"Get her and bring her to the house." Master David ordered as he stalked off to wait for Nance.

# Chapter Six

Ramona fought for the strength to withstand the pain and humiliation of being slung over a horse's saddle like a sack of grain. Her heart leaped in her breast and she felt a sick feeling in her gut, they ain't taking me to General Hopkins place. She knew when they reached the Jonas Plantation that her dreams of freedom were ended. I'm in deep trouble, Where is my God, am I too small for him to notice?

When they reached the front lawn of the Jonas Plantation, Master Jessie and his household slaves were waiting.

There was a low rumble throughout the crowd as she was yank off the horse and slammed onto the ground in front of Master Jessie.

"I laid claim to you, cause I'm the only one who hunted you down and I am the one who brought you back. You belong to me now, the General don't have anything to say from now on, do you understand?"

Master Jessie Jonas strutted around the compound snapping his whip against his thigh, while his eyes examined the terrified girl.

"Tie her to that tree," shouted the half crazed man, "I'll teach her to have some manners when she's dealing with her betters."

Although frightened, Ramona stood tall and proud while Master Jessie walked around her flicking at her clothing with the whip. "You still pure?" He asked.

What is he talking about I was always pure. Pure what? I pure nigger if that's what he's talking about. If he means is I still a girl, then yes, I'm still pure.

"Answer me you black bitch, are you trying to piss me off? When I say I want an answer that means now."

"I don't know what you want me to say, I'm still a girl." Ramona thought for a moment and added, " I ain't had no man, is that what you asking?"

Master Jessie asked "Why did you have to think about your answer, are you trying to fool me?"

"No sir, I just wanted to be sure what you was asking."

"You are going to be punished for running; maybe I'll break both legs," said a grinning Master Jessie, "that should slow you down."

"The terrified girl made up her mind right there and then that Master Jessie would never get her willingly.

"Tie her to the whipping tree, she has to be taught a lesson and I want the rest of you niggers to watch so's you all will know what waits for anybody that runs."

"Two of the men who worked in the fields walked slowly to where Ramona stood bleeding from the small tears in her skin, pulled her to that cursed tree and tied her hands around the trunk with her back facing Master Jessie.

"Master Jessie did the unspeakable act himself; he took great pleasure in every one of the twenty lashes that he gave the mutinous girl. When his arm tired from the brutal beating, he stomped into the house and flopped down in his leather chair and dreamed of his next meeting with Ramona.

"The whipping had exhilarated Master Jessie, his heart was thumping wildly, blood was racing through his veins and his thoughts turned to the hot sweaty body of the child he had just beaten. "Gotta wait, but I'll get her soon," he cautioned himself as he massaged his throbbing penis.

"Two of the slave women untied the beaten child from the bloody whipping tree and carried her to one of the cabins behind the huge house where the Master, his wife lived."

"I being lonely for my friend and terrified over the capture of Ramona fell so sick that I was hidden away from Master David's prying eyes.

"Ever since Master David's humiliation he had become a tormentor of his people. Forgotten was his claim of being their salvation and protection. Everyone felt his wrath. His fury at losing Ramona knew no bounds; he beat the very young women and then used them to satisfy his greedy appetites.

"The black men of the slave community fought to contain their anger. Wives begged their husbands, and lovers plead with their partners not to cause any trouble. Big Fred heard the rumors of rebellion and promptly confiscated all the weapons that were used by the slaves to supplement their diets. Locking the few old battered guns in one of the sheds he tucked the key under the leg of his bunk bed. If there is a rebellion, he thought, I will be in control of the guns. The way things are going I'll need all the help I can get. This place is crazy with fear.

"Sophia waited her chance and when she was sure she could talk without being heard she cornered George and asked straight out, "When you gonna run again?"

"Surprise flashed across his face as he answered her question with a question, "What makes you think I gonna run?""

"Seen too many runners not to know one when I sees one," she answered.

"Why you asking?" he countered.

"Cause I got me a child I want ta send with you if you headin north."

"Now Sophia, why would any damn fool want to take a child with him ifen he on the run?"

"Cause he gonna save the chile's life if he take her with him."

"If a fella was a runner I guess he could take a child along, might make his chances easier, after all, who in their right mind would suspect that the man was a runner and hauling a child."

"Just let me know if you have a mind to run. When you ready I'll fix some victuals for the road."

"George left the two women to their labors while he slyly applauded himself on his good luck, first the food would be welcome and the child for distraction was an added benefit, maybe he could even sell her when he was finished with her."

"He a pretty slippery fella, you sure you doing the right thing?" Ermine hesitated and then continued the question, "You sure to God gonna trust that fella? They say in the quarters that he pesters the little girls to call him Uncle George; I don't trust that sneaky low down Uncle George!"

"With a weary sigh Sophia, asked an important question. Ermine, you ain't blind, what other chance she got?"

"I guess you right, all hell gonna break lose round here pretty soon anyhow."

" It seems George Hanson Phillips, aka Uncle George had made a name for himself in the world of blacks and all knew of his appetite for young girls, as I found out later.

"That bastard say for you to come to the house, he say you had enough time to grieve."

Nance listened intently, her bronze colored eyes widening as Sophia relayed Master David's order.

"I ain't mournful for the child, I'm sorrowful for the Preacher Man and me, we done had a beautiful thing and now it lost. Preacher Man said he loved me and didn't think he could live without me. Well, Master David better find another women to warm his bed, I ain't his whore no more!"

"Since when you have a choice?" Sophia warned, "now be quick and fix yourself before he come looking."

"Glancing back as she headed back to the house, Sophia saw Nance come out of the cabin and head for the field where the despondent girl had recently buried her first child."

"Now what is that girl up to, " Sophia mumbled.

"Nance knelt by the small mound, and fingering the knife that she had begun carrying after her terrifying brush with Master David, she felt a tear run down her cheek. As she plunged the knife deep into her gut, she marveled at the absence of pain, she only felt a deep sadness as she lay seeping into the Georgia earth. She had always known this day was coming and she was prepared. No more was she gonna be used and then thrown away like a used up sack of grain. She was better then that, hadn't the Preacher Man told her so.

"Preacher Man's body was found on bended knee, leaning against the wall as though he had knelt to pray when the angel of death had struck. The blood from the knife wound in his back seeped out onto the wooden floor and stained the scrubbed wood a burnished brown. The neatness of the shack was only scarred by the violent act that had taken place during early morning prayers.

"While making his rounds at sundown, Big Fred found Nance's body. Gently lifting her lifeless corpse he placed her over the saddle and began to walk the horse and its burden back to the master's house. *The poor beast is jittery,* he thought, *It's never been used to carry a body before, well you pitiful beast, get used to it cause this won't be the last time.*"

"With the news of Nance's murder of Henry, her grisly self inflicted death, rage raced through the compound, folks began to filter out of their cabins. The terrible knowledge that Nance had gone mad and sacrificed her life to be free from Master David had been whispered hurriedly from one slave to the next. The message clearly spoke to the angry crowd and contributed to their burning desire to be free from this tyranny."

"Big Fred led the skittish horse and its tragic burden onto Master David's front lawn and as he carefully lifted her slack body from the animal's back, while a crowd gathered.

"The mob of black men and women milling around the lifeless body of Nance turned to aggression, raising their voices in protest. I could smell and taste the hatred, I remember spitting to rid my mouth of that foul taste. One of the men at the front of the crowd began chanting, Master David where you be, your child is dead and so be she. Come and give your women her due after what she been for you."

"Another voice rang out proclaiming, ain't nowhere in this world should a woman have to kill herself to keep from being used. The fact that the beast of a man doing the using is one of our own kind, makes me shamed, it's the final insult!"

"Big Fred had slowly eased his way out of the crowd and guiding the still jittery horse to the edge of the lawn he slid behind a stand of trees and watched, as the crowd grew angrier. Their smoldering rage destroyed the restraints of abject fear and the crowd moved as one. Storming the house, the uncontrolled mass of oppressed human vindicators began smashing and burning everything in sight.

"Heading to his cabin, where he had stashed the guns he picked out the best one for himself. Big Fred then ran for the barn. Saddling and mounting the fastest horse, he rode off the property leaving the mayhem behind.

"Master David saw Big Fred as he rode away and cursed the man for leaving him defenseless. Sneaking down the back stairs, Master David made his way to the barn where the horses were kept and sliding into the darkened building, he began saddling a horse when they stepped out of the shadows. Two of the men that he had treated so badly over the years stood between him and the open door to the barn.

"Where you going Master David, they's work to be done, cotton to be picked and weighed, then there's the bagging." The smiling black man licked his full lips and pushed his former master with such force that he fell to the ground. "Can't have you getting off slacking your work. You gonna need this here pitch fork for some of your work, did you see how sharp it is? Why it can go right through a man's leg and not hurt a bit. Ain't that what you told me when it happened to me. Didn't you made me work twice as hard for trying to slack off with a little scratch?"

"Show him how sharp it really is Seth," Toby egged on the other man who had waited in the barn with him, "give him the same treatment as he gave you."

"Master David lay on the ground frozen with fear, now he was going to have to face off two of the people he had bullied for years. Searching their faces for some flicker of humanity, he found none."

"Sophia had sneaked down to the barn and seen the stand off with Master David and the two men, but she kept coming to where I was hiding. She knew that now was the only time to get me out of harms way. I prayed that master wouldn't see her and whip her for helping me escape. I was huddled in a corner of the barn; my hair had been chopped off so I looked like a boy. The only thing that gave me away was my dress. I was shivering even though the dress was wet with sweat."

"Come child we got to get you outta here before all hell breaks loose. I brought this pair of britches and shirt for you. You gonna be a boy for a while.

"As she talked she was pulling me from the hot humid barn into the fresh clean air of the yard."

The fires that had been set around the great house would surely bring the white men, and when black folks and white folks meet it was always the unlucky black folks that paid.

"In the distance I could see men on horses and following them were wagons carrying men from the village."

Pushing me into the woods Sophia tossed the clothing in my direction and ordered me to change.

"She said, "I'll be back later, after I find George, he gonna take you with him to the north.""

"I could only solemnly nod my head. I waited and waited, day turned into night and still I waited. I'd seen the men from town come and I had heard the gunshots, but no one came for me. When the men finally rode away I knew that no one would come.

"Walking back to the great house I saw the bodies of Sophia and George laying in the courtyard. They had been stripped and beaten to death, the rest of the slave's bodies were scattered over most of the grounds. The children I had watched playing games of tag and kick the gourd were piled together as though sharing some horrible new game.

"I searched in vain for a live person to help me bury the dead. Full of fear and shock I made my way into the barn where I found Master David. He was pinned to the earth with pitchforks through both arms. He had slowly bled to death. I saw the two black men near Master David their heads had been blasted from their bodies. I remember thinking, they didn't cut their heads off, they tore their heads off. In a daze I wandered from the dusty barn out of into the sweltering hot yard with its smell of gunpowder and blood rising like waves in an ocean. This horror was too much for any human to bear and I began to vomit. That's all I can remember."

"This is the scene the itinerant preacher found when he first came upon the massacre. A small child standing in a blood spattered yard staring at nothing. He being a self appointed man of God was pressed to try and save this poor lost child. Taking me to his canvas covered wagon he settled me into a makeshift bed in the back of his wagon. I obeyed as though I had no will, too much violence; too much violence had left me in a stupor. He gave me a drink of his magic elixir and I slept for hours. Later I found out it was a mixture of berries and grain brewed separately then combined and by adding a sweetener it became a very potent concoction that the preacher claimed would cure anything from gout to hair loss."

"The raiders had loaded most of the belonging that they thought were valuable and hauled it into town to be shared later. The preacher being a sensible man concluded that these dead people would no longer need the things of this earth, but, as he told me later, a man on the move preaching God's word could use them to make life a little easier.

"His great height and plain black clothing that he had adopted as the right garb for a preacher were the only things that set him apart from any other farmer working the land. Tossing aside his frayed black waistcoat and large brimmed black hat, he began the job of recycling the goods. His finely chiseled face was lined with creases of smoke from the still smoldering fires; the white beard he wore to inspire confidence was streaked with soot from the articles that he had confiscated.

"While I slept he had searched through the rubble for anything that was still usable. He had seen the bodies scattered about, but decided there was too many for him to bury and God have provided a perfect way to reprocess the bodies. What the animals didn't eat or drag away the earth would use as fertilizer.

"Glancing up at the huge birds waiting in the closest trees the preacher gave a shudder and continued his search. Making several trips through the once stately house he had gathered a pile of blankets and any edible foodstuffs that could be hoarded for the lean days that he knew were coming. He hastily stored the booty in the wagon and shaking his head, marveled at my ability to sleep through the noise of packing the goods neatly in the wagon. After all, he later told me that there was only so much room in that wagon and it had to be kept orderly.

"The preacher was wise in hurrying; the men in the posse had unloaded their first load of plunder and were riding back for the rest of the goods. If they caught him they would be angry about losing out on the things he had liberated and doubly outraged at the preacher for giving aid to a slave. That was against the law."

"I guess Ned Horton wanted to be a slave owner and owning a slave would put him up a peg in society, or so he thought. Age doesn't count when your black. I was either owned by some body or up for grabs.

"We suspected that his bunch of hooligans followed him only because he bullied them or coaxed them with a jug of moonshine. One of his men was heard remarking to another of the group.

"That fool wants to own a slave, never mind that he can't feed his wife and kids, he wants to feel rich and powerful. What a laugh!"

"Glancing toward town the preacher saw a cloud of dust and knew that it was time to leave. Grabbing his gun from inside the wagon he jumped up on the driver's seat and whipped the ass of the aging horse until it burst toward the woods. He made it to the tree line just in time; the men from town had arrived on the scene and were searching the cabins.

"This preacher was a man who never missed an opportunity to get ahead in this world. He was often heard saying, "God's word will sustain me, but a fellow never should miss a chance to give God a hand."

"Two old maid aunts, who had taught him to read the bible and pray to a vindictive God for forgiveness for imagined sins, had raised preacher John Cavendish.

"They had disowned their brother, John's father, Floyd Cavendish when he had gotten the girl from the next farm pregnant and they had thrown their young brother out to fend for himself. Floyd had married the lovely Julie and three months later John was born. John's memories of the next few years was a blur of jobs in strange towns, Papa coming home drunk, Mama entertaining strange men, and finally the fire that took their lives.

"John at a very early age had begun hanging around the tavern waiting for the drunks to come out; they usually gave him a coin to get rid of his annoying nasal badgering. He had learned early on that people were tired of beggars, but they would pay something to get rid of an annoyance. He used those few coins to buy food and his favorite treat, licorice sticks.

"He spent most of his evening outside the tavern hustling drunks and when he heard the fire bell ran toward the sound of the crowd shouting. To his horror the shack where Papa, Mama, and he had been living was now going up in smoke and flames.

"When Sheriff Foster realized that John wasn't in the shack with his parents, he grabbed him by the ear hauled, him to the jail and locked him in a cell.

"The sheriff had known John's father as a boy; he also knew the sisters and their father when he and his family had lived on the farm next to the Cavendish's. He sent a telegram to the sisters telling them that he was sending their ten-year-old nephew on the next train.

"The Cavendish sisters had lived a solitary life; the only people they ever saw were the people they hired to work the farm, which barely eked out a living. Their first and only love was this house that their father had built with his own hands and they had worshiped both their father and this house.

"They were cold and distant with the boy when he first came to live with them and he hated them. By pretending to pray for forgiveness every time he committed some so called sin; he soon learned how to manipulate the ecstatic sisters.

Putting John's name on the deed had been a covenant between the sisters and John, he was to keep the house and land and pass it on to his children When the sisters died he sold the farm, got drunk, had a women, and used the money that was left to buy his wagon, his home on wheels. He was well versed in scripture and knew he could earn a living preaching to other folks about the wages of sin.

# Chapter Seven

In those days, Lorri honey, our only way of finding out what happened to our loved ones was through the grapevine, folks were being bought and sold all the time and news of kin went with them. Sometimes we heard the stories right away, but most times we heard it years later and that's how I heard the news of Ramona.

"Back at the Jessie Jonas Plantation Ramona's body had recovered from the whipping, but her mind had turned vicious. She fought all attempts to help her. Her face was no longer beautiful and serene, there were lines of madness etched around the eyes, and her once lovely succulent mouth was a cold, grim line stretched across her face. She involuntarily shuddered and screamed when touched by human hands; Ramona's life was a living hell. Master Jessie Jonas had tried to take her to his bed after her body had healed, but her terrified screaming had alerted Master Jessie's usually dull witted wife, and she had come running into his den and demanded to know why the girl was screaming and why she was still in the house at this late hour."

"If times had been different, Master Jessie would have had Ramona killed for rejecting him, but every one in these parts had heard of the uprising at the Master David's plantation, and he wasn't about to get these niggers riled up. Now to add to his frustration, he had to make sure that nothing bad happened to Ramona.

"Master Jessie continued to take out his frustrations on the household staff, but they cautiously wore satisfied smiles and actually grinned when they were out of his sight. Their delight in seeing this white man experience a small part of the rage they lived with every day was a balm to their captured spirits."

"Preacher John Cavendish had never had a solitary soul depending on him before and I think he relished the idea that he was in control of another person's life. In his youth he had always been controlled by others, first his drunken parents, then the unfeeling aunts, and lastly by the sheriff in whose jail he had spent three weeks locked up for drunkenness. The two years that him and me had spent traveling around the country was a boon to this complex man, for he had grown to love me, and I him. He was content to have me sitting quietly by his side while he drove from town to town. Even though I had to crawl into the wagon and hide whenever we came to a town, his heart was also proud of me and yearned to show me off to his audience. Playing God to me, who he had to hide all the time was not fulfilling, he had even debated turning me in for the reward money.

"After all, he told me that I would be able to live a life in the light of day not hide every time someone came near the wagon. The idea that I would spend the rest of my life at the beck and call of strangers did not sit well with him either. The only solution he could come up with was to take me to see Lily, a woman who he had met during his wanderings. She lived down in Baton Rouge where the color of your skin wasn't quite so important."

"Lilly had been his first long time lover, and was a kind soul with a good and generous heart. The golden-haired haired Lilly with her alabaster skin had been a beauty in her younger days, and the many years of living her life on the fringes of society had not taken a heavy toll. The few wrinkles that were sprinkled near her lovely blue eyes only served to enhance her gentle features. Lilly St James was still a handsome woman and she still welcomed her Preacher John with open arms."

"When John had finished explaining his plan for her to keep and raise me as her own. She shook her head in denial, "Honey, what am I going to do with a half grown girl and a black one at that? If she was lighter or mulatto I could say she was mine, but she's so dark they going to know she isn't any part of me."

"Lilly, you know people, get her some papers," John whispered eagerly, "ain't nobody gonna be looking for her anyway."

" I suppose I could talk to a couple of people. I'm not promising anything but I'll try. What is this girl to you anyhow," asked Lilly?

"Her heart leaped in her breast as she watched John's eyes soften when he talked about me, a gangly ten years old.

"She later told me, that she just knew from his facial expression that John Cavendish loved me like I was his own. Her heart had agreed with this troubled man and she silently vowed to do her best to fulfill his wishes.

"When the papers that claimed Jessie as her chattel were drawn up and signed by a very high official in the town, Preacher John prepared to get back on the road. Lilly had tried to talk him into staying with her and Jessie, but he had the soul of a gypsy. The road with its siren call was not to be denied. While

Preacher John was unpacking my few belongings from the wagon, I stood watching, my blank dark eyes had long since faded into what the Preacher John now called a warm honey color. Now I could feel them filling with tears. I felt that I would never see Preacher John again. My only friend was leaving me with a white stranger. A sick feeling stole over me and I longed for the days when I was back with Ramona, Sophia and the all the folks from Master David's Plantation."

"Lilly took my hand and held it as John jumped up on the driver's seat, grabbed the reigns and hurriedly left. Standing in front of the pink adobe hacienda we watched Preacher John Cavendish drive out of our lives."

# Chapter Eight

Day by day my respect and trust for my benefactor grew; Lilly's gentle, happy outlook on life crept into my heart and I finally felt as though I had come home. Our mother, daughter relationship began to bloom when Lilly employed a creative Creole woman from the local dressmaker's shop to measure me for a new wardrobe. Until now, my only clothing had been the cotton shift that I wore and the grain sack under drawers that covered my bottom. I had taken to washing them every night so they would be fresh and clean by morning.

The two women giggled and laughed at my antics while I paraded around the room strutting like I had seen those haughty Creole women do as they strolled by the villa. When finished the creative women had fashioned several gowns that perfectly fit my budding young body.

Teaching me to be proud of my heritage was one of Lilly's first goals.

"Child, you are a lovely, gentle girl and you must teach others how to treat you," advised Lilly, "if you don't respect yourself how can you expect others to?"

"Lilly completely adored me even though I was a shy, distrustful child. She vowed to make my life as easy as she could manage. Slowly but surely Lilly taught me to grow as a person. The days of happiness and contentment wound around us casting a spell of hope for both. Teaching me to sew a fine seam and to read a book was as exciting to Lilly as her own first adventure with the written word. She taught me to use the homemade pomade that kept my frizzy hair from flying in the wind. She had carefully mixed the many herbs and spices that had grown in her garden and lastly stirred in some rendered fat in it for consistency. But the most important lesson she taught me was that the word 'nigger' was just a word to describe a black person when used by whites. They used the word to dehumanize the black man and was a hurtful insult of the highest degree. It became a venomous, bitter word that folks full of hate spewed out like the deadly garbage that it was. Here again the white folks made up a word and turned it against us."

"Fate has a way of catching up with everyone and my time had come.

"While Lilly was busy planning a party for what I thought was my fifteenth birthday the frightening news came! Senior Franklin was dead!

"Senior Theodore Franklin had been brought to New Orleans when he was a child and his love for this vibrant city had grown with each passing year. As a young man he was fascinated with the diverse collection of people, the many different languages, and the stimulating hodgepodge of architecture. When he had made a comfortable fortune, he had built two Spanish Haciendas, one for his own home and one for Lilly, the women he had grown to love. His estranged wife had rebelled against living in what she called a Mexican hovel, but when he had suggested that if she didn't think she could live in their home with him, she was free to go back to England where she could feel more comfortable, she had changed her mind.

"Miranda Franklin, a beautifully cold woman, aloofly informed her husband that she would remain here but only as a guest.

"Don't expect any sort of personal contact from me," she had informed her grateful husband. Miranda played the rejected wife for a whole month and then began taking lovers. She liked them young, dark skinned, and very submissive. Her reputation as a generous lover soon grew and she had no problem replacing her young lovers as she tired of them."

"I had no way of knowing that Lilly's way of life was precarious to say the least, her male friend who had commissioned the building of Lilly's hacienda had been shot in a duel and Miranda Franklin, the surviving wife did not intend to support his illicit lover."

"The widow Franklin had known about the liaison between her husband and Lilly for years and had condoned it. She had reasoned that Lilly was the compensated recipient of her husband's attentions, his personal whore, but now she was playing the martyr and insisting that Lilly had stolen her husband's love. She demanded that her husband's consort move out of the house that he had long ago given to Lilly. Mrs. Franklin even had the audacity to insist to anyone who would listen, that Lilly and her ilk should be forced to leave town.

"The community began ostracizing the once socially acceptable Lilly. One morning her cook came running in as fast as her huge bulk would permit and complained, about the green grocer refusing to bring the order of the day. He was the man who had delivered her fruits and vegetables for many years and Lilly had always considered him a friend.

"Her needlepoint group had withdrawn their invitation to the competition for best tapestry of the month. And to add insult to injury the local sheriff

*JESSIE'S FLIGHT TO FREEDOM*

announced his intention to check the papers of one Jessie Jonas, the so called maid to Miss Lilly LaFountain.

"Rumor had it that Mrs. Franklin was now shopping around for an assassin to eliminate her challenger for the hacienda and the land that went with it. When Lilly heard this news through the grapevine she hurriedly began to pack. Shouting for me she ordered me to pack only what was needed and meet her at the edge of the public square.

"I have quite a sum of money stashed away with a friend here in town. I'll go collect it and a buggy and meet you there at dusk. Now promise you will wait there for me."

"I nodded my head in agreement, but I could feel the fear creeping back into my gut. I knew that I was gonna be alone just like always. Can't get too happy it ain't in the cards for me."

"As I readied myself for the trip I began to hum some of the old gospels that Ramona had taught me. If only I could see Ramona again, I remember whispering as I stared at the blank wall.

"With heavy heart I followed Lilly's instructions and waited for my friend who would never come. After many hours of fruitless waiting I tried to think of a place where Lilly would search for me and I settled on the church as my sanctuary. My thoughts flew to the adobe chapel that Lilly had worshiped in every morning since I had known her. Making my way to the church, I hid in one of the empty pews of that that cold empty chapel, and I fervently prayed for Lilly's safe return. My eyes were getting heavy and my head kept dipping low into the front of my soft green sateen gown. I could smell the scent of oleander wafting up from between my breast and it lulled me into a stage of contentment until I felt myself nodding off to sleep."

"Two women entered the quiet church. They wore black shawls covering their heads and the long black bereavement dresses that was the expected garb of a surviving widow. They had come to pray and light candles for their loved ones and the sound of their voices breaking the silence pulled me back from the serene state I had entered. I scurried into a pew and sat with bowed head listening while they talked.

The oldest women said, "Did you hear about Lilly LaFountain being found at the edge of the town with her throat slit?"

"Cold fear settled into my gut and turned to stone. I had this sudden urge to pee, but was afraid to move."

"Yes," answered the other woman, "and I heard that it was a hired job but try and prove it. Whoever did the deed had rifled through her belongings and stolen everything of value, so now their saying it was a robbery."

"Not in my book!" answered the first women, "you know that Franklin woman, and she would do anything to protect her little kingdom. She knew about Lilly for years and did nothing cause it kept her own middle-aged husband out of her bed. That bitch has had many lovers you know and she has the guts to try and blemishes Lilly's good name. Well, someday that sheriff is going to catch up with her and her shady deals, you mark my words."

"Hush up, and act contrite," shushed the second woman.

"Good morning Father," she said bowing her head and then she added, "I'm here for confession and to receive communion."

"Come my child I will hear your confession," answered the local priest as he led the woman to the side of the church where the confessionals were located.

"Father Simian knew these two parishioners very well and loved them with a forgiving heart and prayed for their redemption at the same time."

"I sat there crushed; my friend was dead and in such a horrible way. I pictured the men I had seen in the barn with their heads shot off and my stomach began to heave.

"Come with me child," whispered a strained voice, "we have got to get out of here before that bitch finds out where you are and comes for you too."

"My eyes searched the church behind me until I found the owner of the voice. John John Rodriquez was standing plastered against the arch that separated the entrance of the chapel from the magnificent altar.

"I'm Lilly's friend and you can call me John John," he hissed, "I'm the one who was holding her money for her. Come with me and hurry, we are meeting another friend and we can't be late."

"How did you know who I was? I questioned, suspecting it to be a trap."

"Honey you're the only one that fits Lilly's description, she said to watch for a 'little black angel,' and you sure seem to fill the bill."

"This nearly empty house of worship echoed eerily with every sound. Should I trust this man who says he is Lilly's friend, should I scream for help, or should I run, the questions sent waves of fear racing through my body."

"To me, heavy eyed from lack of sleep the stranger's voice sounded sincere and besides I had nowhere to run. Quietly I slipped from the pew and followed the stranger through a settlement of rundown shacks and silent hungry children. I hadn't realized that there were poor white folks until now. The path began to get smoother as we reached a wall that surrounded a large plantation at the edge of town."

"John John told me that this place got lots of black slaves, they won't notice one more if you slip in at night. You can stay here till your friend the preacher comes for you. I sent word that Lilly was dead and that you needed him. Now mix in with the others and I will be back in a couple of days to check on you."

"No, I am not going to be a slave again," I protested.

"Baby, you gonna be just fine here with me," came a deep vibrant voice from the other side of the wall.

"Out from behind a nearby tree stepped the handsomest man I had ever seen. His broad shoulders and slim waist told me that he wasn't just any ordinary man. When he flashed me that conspirator's grin, I was almost blinded by his dazzling smile. He wore tattered white work clothes like most of the pickers, but he had cut off his pants legs just below the knee allowing the huge muscles in his legs to flex as he walked. The superb condition of his body spoke of years of long hard labor."

"You 'all come with me sweet thang, we gonna make sure you safe."

"I went weak with desire, who was this man that he should trouble me so? I forgot I had to pee, I forgot everything except staying close to this man.

"Lorrie, when he said spoke to me, my goose bumps had goose bumps. It made me glad that I was a woman. I followed that beautiful man. I had completely forgotten about John John, who, I was later to find out was quite used to being ignored when Edward King was around."

*"What is going on, why am I feeling these quivers? He ain't nothing but another black man that totes for the white man,* I thought. *I questioned my feelings all the way to the hut that I thought was going to be my temporary home."*

"Shug, this gonna be your home for a while, you gonna share with Miss liddy, she got several, ah, you can call them nieces living with her and they gonna treat you good. They in the field now but when they come in you tell them that I say so."

"When he left that doorway my world got a little darker, like my sun was gone behind a cloud. You know, you'd a thought I'd a had a suspicion even back then. Well, when Miss liddy and her nieces came in from the fields, it was pretty plain what they were up to. Their clothes weren't grubby from labor, but they had a stink of sweat, urine, and something foul.

"I could almost always smell that same stench after Senior Theodore Franklin had come to visit Miss Lilly, of course she was always quick to bath and freshen up. I knew that for them, their time alone was sharing of each other body and soul. Such were the deep feelings between the two of them so that made it seem all right in my book. I vowed right then that this little gal wasn't gonna end up doing whatever it was these gals were doing.

"Miss Liddy come over to me and touched my cheek saying, "You ain't nothing but a chile, you can't stay here. The other gals are gonna expect you to work too."

"I mouthed her right back and told her, "I ain't doing what you doing, they can kill me first."

"She just laughed and told me that I could stay the night but I had to find another place tomorrow. I had a hard time falling asleep in that new place. When I was almost asleep I heard sniffling from one of the girls, then another girl joined her and I knew they weren't happy about their jobs either."

"When the sun came up the girls just lay there talking and planning what they gonna do after they get free. Like that was ever gonna happen!

"I heard the workers leave for the fields and I dozed back off to sleep. When I woke up again the girls were gone, it seems they had to be at the work site when the men broke for lunch. The workers had fifteen minutes to eat and rest and the girls had to be there in case someone didn't want to eat or rest.

"Miss Liddy told me later that this master bragged that his men didn't run away, they ran to his place. Keep em happy, well fed, and satisfied was his saying."

"While the girls were out doing what they had to do, I cleaned up the place. It hadn't been swept in days and the one window that was in the place was so dirty it didn't let the sun in at all. My friend Miss Lilly had taught me that cleanliness is next to Godliness and I believed her. When the girls come back from the fields they noticed the clean cabin right away and praised me for my work.

"Let her stay," the girls had begged Miss Liddy, "we can all share the food and she will be safe here," they had promised.

"Well let me tell you I was hoping she would let me stay too. Then I could see that handsome devil, Edward King again."

I could see that telling her story was helping Jessie, but it also was draining her energy from an already weakened body. She had been through so much pain in the last few years and still she fought death.

I suggested she eat some of the soup that I had made for her, get some rest and save the rest of the story until morning when she would be better rested. Propping her up on pillows I checked to be sure the soup wasn't too warm and slowly brought the spoon to her grimly stretched lips. She bravely sipped a couple spoonfuls of the warm liquid and fell back onto the pillows

"You're right, Lorrie I got to rest for just a bit, but not all the way to morning. I gotta get it off my mind and I want the world to know what kind of life we had. I'll just snooze for a speck and then I'll tell you about my first love."

With a grin forced from God knows where she slipped into the past."
I quietly watched as Jessie's impish grin faded to an open mouthed snore. I could feel my heart swell with pride for that child that she had been, and for the women she had become. As Jessie slept, I remembered the many happy days in Haven Place, Kate had run it, Sadie and I and many others worked in the house. Harrison was our pimp, our mentor, our friend and so much more. He taught us to respect ourselves, and not to hate the men who came to buy our bodies. Strange as it may seem to outsiders we were family. The parties were wonderful and the friendly teasing sustained us through the bad times.

Jessie had kept that house together with her bossy ways, good common sense, and the fact that she cooked like an angel. Most of all I remember the welcoming, everyday calm that prevailed when Jessie hummed or sang a hymn. She had made that house a home and we didn't even appreciate her until we were losing her. I didn't want to stop praying for a miracle, but I didn't want to prolong her life if she had to suffer so horribly. I waited for God to make the decision, after all that is His job not mine.

After an hour had gone by she began to stir, I held out a glass of water and then offered her a spoonful of Laudanum.

"No honey, I want my last hours to be as clear as this damn pain will let them be.

"Have you ever seen a man and knew he was supposed to be yours for all your life? No? Well I did. I knew that Edward was supposed to be mine from before time ever began. I could feel him in me before he ever touched me. My heart was his the minute I saw him and when he spoke to me in his deep vibrant voice I went weak with desire. I didn't know what it was I wanted but whatever it was, it was with him. He gave me such pleasure when he finally made me his own. I just knew that we would live to grow old together."

Even after all these years when Jessie remembered Edward King, her face took on a glow that was almost saintly. She had truly loved that heart-breaking cad and still wouldn't face the fact that some men are born to trifle with any girl's feelings.

"The hiding from the master, the sharing of Miss liddy's house and food all were unimportant to me, I was Edward's woman. He always called me his little bird cause he said I didn't weigh as much as the birds in the treetops, he would laugh, squeeze me hard and say, thats why they can set on a branch and bend with the wind."

"I thought it was a silly love name but later I realized he was preparing me for the bending part. Edward liked women, all women, but he especially liked gals with meat on their bones. He said it gave him something to hang on to.

"After a wonderful spring of hiding and loving, the charm was broken he began to stay away. I begged him to tell me what was wrong but he couldn't answer."

She paused in her story and with a thoughtfully sad look murmured, "I don't think he ever knew either;"

Jessie's eyes filled with tears as she added, "Maybe he needed something I couldn't give him.

"When I began to put some meat on my bones he came back but only till he found out why I was gaining. I was gonna have his child, then he was gone again.

"All the while the girls who were staying in Liddy's cabin kept warning me to stay out of the fields they said I was not likely to have this child if I kept on working under the hot sun, but in my heart I knew God wouldn't let anything happen to this gift of love that Edward had given me. Boy, did I find out that God has different plans for this wayward child. When my baby came into this world he came out screaming and crying, just the way Tilda said I did. That baby was too early; I guess he couldn't wait to meet his mama."

The sadness crept back onto Jessie's face as she remembered her first and only child.

"I lost that child when I was in my eighth month, I never had another one, but the weight stayed on and back came Edward. I was thankful that he came back to me, but I yearned for the child we had lost. It made me crazy when he run around with some of the other gals but down deep I knew he was mine. He was just sowing some wild oats. That man could work all day and love all night. He sure was something! Hell on wheels and I still miss the feel of him. She sighed.

"That master acted like he was above us and didn't take up boogering the gals, but his sons sure did. His oldest son by the name of Fredrick had his favorite gal and she was always happy to accommodate him, she strutted her stuff when he was around. That damned cocky girl liked him and we were glad cause it meant extra food and lots of yard goods for dresses. That was a good time for us."

"You know I never could remember Fredrick's daddy's name, to remember his son's name, but not his. Ain't that funny, he bossed our lives and I can't even remember his name?

"Meanwhile my man, Edward King got to fooling around with first one then another of the gals in our camp. He never seemed to pick a special gal except me. I was still with him near every night so it damned near drove me wild when I caught him with other women."

Jessie paused in her story, her eyes stared back to that time, her small pain wracked body was motionless with anticipation as though she still expected to see Edward coming to her.

"That hell went on for nigh onto three years." Jessie continued. "I really think that old master knew I was hiding there but pretended he didn't see me."

Jessie looked me straight in the eye and asked, " Lorrie do you know what it's like to have someone look through you? I felt like I was a ghost in those days, the only time I was real is when I was with Edward. My heart was full to bursting when he showed up one night with a pair of bright red shoes, that and the child were the only gifts he ever gave me.

"When that bitch came along and stole my Edward away I even thought of killing myself, that's how desperate I was for his love.

"Edward wasn't coming to me anymore; he was spending his nights with that raggedy assed runaway dancer. She was skinny as a rat and just as sneaky. Damn her soul, she began wearing bright red shoes too!

"Now, all my nights were spent with the gals from Miss Liddy's. We gossiped and sang hymns, combed and braided each other's hair, pretending we were mistresses of our own plantations where we were happy and free to live like we wanted."

"One lonely night when I couldn't take it no more I went to Edward and begged him to tell me what I could do to win him back. Foolish child that I was I thought I could change enough to make him love me again.

" He heaved himself off the bench where he had sitting and stretched up to his full height. Standing tall with his strong legs planted wide, muscles rippling in his sculptured arms, and with a face full of anger, he spat out these hateful words.

"Women, you too white! I needs a high stepping gal that talk our talk, not whitey talk, you way too highfalutin for me."

"Even then I thought he was beautiful, here he was tearing my heart from my body and he still seemed like a God to me. I can still see him standing tall, full of pride, tearing me down for being me. Well let me tell you I learned to talk the way the others talked in a damned hurry just thinking I could get my man back."

"The education that I had gotten from Miss Lilly and Preacher John Cavendish had given me was tossed aside for that man. I never did go back to my old way of talking until now. That new way of talking was another way for me to keep passing as one of the slaves on the plantation. At first it was fun, then it became my way of life."

Jessie laughed derisively, and added, "Edward never did come back to me, but I kept him damn busy running from me. He finally got so fed up with my badgering that he took that bitch and lit out for a small new town that we had only heard of. The name of the town was Freedom and it was the only place that we have ever heard of that was run by black folks only. If you made it to the town you were free, the other folks that already lived there didn't let nobody, black or white, come slave hunting.

"Later we found out that a band of clansmen raided the town and set it afire, the folks from the town never did rebuild. It had been a free town for five years and was the only one I ever heard of that lasted that long. Seems the white folks that lived nearby were afraid that their slaves would rebel and get ideas when they saw all that freedom. They couldn't have their bought and paid for property getting uppity! Well let me tell you my was heart broken when I found out that Edward was gone, I planned, schemed, then decided to follow him. My head was not working right or I would have known that you couldn't force anybody to love you."

# Chapter Nine

When I left Miss Liddy's place all the girls cried, but not for long, they were down with some kind of sickness that was eating at their women parts. I think they were glad I was leaving before I got sick too. I was glad to be getting away from all that nasty disgusting odor; it reminded me of the long ago barnyard where Preacher John Cavendish found me. That barnyard had been filled with rotting bodies and the odor of death.

"I lit out that night after everybody had gone to bed, the moon was bright enough to see by and it reminded me of the nights when me and Ramona was on the run. My heart was always sad about never being able to save her from that beast. Oh, I know there isn't much a child can do to save anybody but their own selves, but you still hurt from not trying.

"Times were changing, black folks were fighting back, and white folks were getting scared of the strength we were gaining, so they weren't out riding in packs searching for runaways when I took off. I moved by night and hide by day. Sometimes I was just pure lucky and I'd meet black folks along the way. They would feed me, let me rest, and point me toward the town of freedom."

" It took me about three weeks on the trail of those good-for-nothings, but I finally reached the outskirts of the town of Freedom. I knew that the place to look was where ever they sold hooch. Edward had taken to drink when he started up with that bitch.

"When I hit town I asked the first person I seen about a place to get a drink of hooch. He was an old man with a million wrinkles and rotted teeth. He grinned at me and told me that I best look in Tommy John's place right down the street. I looked in that direction and saw a man going into a rundown shack He grinned and told me he would see me there later on.

"I stared at his back as he shuffled down the dirt road; he was so old and so drunk I wondered if he would ever make it back. He thought I was a whore; cause good girls didn't drink hooch. Oh, I knew what he meant about coming back but I knew that I could never be with that old man or any other man. I belonged to Edward. I found the fella that made hooch and sold it, and my asking about Edward got a big laugh from him and the others in the shack.

"Tommy John was the man's name, a smarty assed black man with slicked back hair and a grin that said he had heard and seen it all. His skinny ass stood grinning and wiping that board that he used for a bar. The soiled rag that he was using was probably leaving filth instead of taking it off. His face held that same sly smile that his cronies were wearing. That smile told me I wasn't going to get any sympathy here.

"When I asked about Edward he stared at me and with a malicious grin he shouted out so all of the other regulars could hear, "That foxy devil, Edward and Miss Flossy done run off to the swamps when they heard yo was comin."

"When they go?" I asked.

"That would be bout two weeks ago and we ain't heard nothing from em since, course folks sometimes disappear for years in that big old swamp. I wouldn't give a care if I was you, he come back when he ready, course it might take some time cause he sure does think Miss Flossy is fine. Why don yo stick aroun here till they come back, I gives yo free drinks," as he set a full glass on that timber that he used for a bar.

"My heart dropped when I heard how long they had been gone into that dark, treacherous rough country. I was so mad I picked up that dammed glass and drank the burning stuff all the way down. Must have been punishing myself for something cause it sure as hell smart that first time. The second drink didn't sting as much and the third didn't sting at all.

"Honey, the thought hit me like a ton of bricks, all of a sudden things didn't look so bad, I could out wait them right here in this friendly place with all the free drinks I wanted.

"I took to drink like a duck takes to water, it were the only thing that kept me from chasing that man into that big old swamp. Well, I should have known it were too good to last, as soon as I was hooked good and sound Tommy John stopped the free drinks! Said I drank too much, I was on my own."

"By this time I was sleeping in the woods back of Tommy John's shack and hustling the regulars for booze. I had stopped caring if I was clean or had food. All I wanted was that next drink.

"I took to sleeping round with anybody for the price of a jug of hooch. It didn't matter who it was, they all looked the same, smiling faces and swollen pricks. The day that I woke up in my little patch of woods and saw that I'd been rolling around the ground with that old man I'd met when I first came into town

*JESSIE'S FLIGHT TO FREEDOM*

that was the day I swore off booze forever. When I saw that ugly old face grinning down at me, with his pecker inside my body, his loose flabby lips and rotted teeth nuzzling my neck I came to my senses. My fuzzy brain asked me, girl what the hells are you doing to yourself? I pushed that greasy, drunken bum off me, rolled over and puked."

Her memories dragged Jessie back to the past and while I sat waiting for her return I tried to picture her drunk, filthy, and timid with anybody. I couldn't draw that picture in my mind, Jessie had always been a strong women and the image of a weak foolish female didn't fit. Her voice tinged with anger startled me back from my imaginings when she returned to her story.

"I had sunk as low as a snake and that feeling wasn't pretty! When my thinking got straight I knew that even if Edward did come back he wouldn't want the towns leavings anyhow. I made up my mind to find work that would keep me in food and clothing; my dress was in rough shape from months of wear and my not bothering to wash it. The duffel with my few changes of clothes that I had brought with me was lost somewhere in that fog of drunkenness. Oh I tell you I was in pretty sad shape but I knew I could get sober and hoped I could stay that way. I made my way down to the creek and went in that icy water clothes and all. Cleaning the smell of that filthy old man off me was the first thing I did, then the smell of puke was next. I was shaking from the cold water, my teeth were chattering, but by God I never felt better in my life!"

"Miss Imogene Smith took me into her boarding house and gave me a cot to sleep on. I was to help her cook and clean for my room and board and that's what I did for the next two years. She warned me when she was thinking about hiring me, "No drinking or whoring while you live here, I won't have you giving me or my place a bad name"

"It seemed so good to be able to do my work and when my chores were done go anywhere I pleased. I took to visiting Emma Mae Washington the local dressmaker and we soon were real good friends. She was good enough a friend for me to tell her my story. We all had a story in those days but when she heard mine she cried."

"Miss Emma was only a few years older then me but she took to mothering me like I was her own chick. She made me a new dresses and some fine hats to match. I was wearing one of those fine hats to the Sunday Meeting when I met Rafe. He was a gentle man with soft brown eyes, that's what you noticed first about him were those wonderful eyes. His tender hands cupped mine and a delighted smile slid across his face when Miss Emma introduced us. I tell you didn't nobody look at me like that in a long time and it sure made me feel good.

"When I told Miss Emma how he made me feel, she just laughed and said, 'Rafe makes everybody feel that way, but don't get any ideas bout him he fancies the men, to bad too cause he sure would be a good catch for some gal, he got brains, money, and he's purty too.'

"Me and Rafe got to be good friends anyway, he would close his store at six, meet me at the corner of the square and we'd walk to Miss Emma's place together. She always had tea and some kind of goodies waiting for us. We would talk for hours bout everything on Gods green earth. Rafe was delighted when he found out I could read. He lent me books and poetry and we would discuss them while Miss Emma, who could neither read nor write, just sat and listened. Those were such joyful times for me.

"Saturday came around and Miss Emma, Rafe, and me had plans for a picnic on the greenest hill outside of town. There were woods nearby for shade and the light breeze promised a pleasant day. The sun was shinning bright; a few white clouds were in that soft blue sky like a giant sea with a one or two tiny sheep playing across its face. I remember thinking, it's a pretty day. I had worn the silky flowered dress Miss Emma had just finished making for me the night before and I felt like a princes

"We spread the blanket while Miss Emma unpacked the lunch. Fried chicken, still warm biscuits, pickled watermelon rinds, and my favorite, Miss Emma's sourdough pancakes spread with honey and current jelly then rolled up like a cigar. She always cut them into fancy little circles. You could see the dark jelly soaking into those golden cakes and that smell would send you to heaven. I ain't had anything as good before or since. I tried making them but they never were the same as Miss Emma's or maybe it was just the times together that I savored.

"Well no matter, after we'd eaten most of that delicious food and packed the soiled dishes back into the nearly empty basket we lay back on the blanket to rest and talk. The conversation always went the same, gossip about work, people, and our hopes and dreams."

"Five white men jumped out of the trees and attacked us, grabbing Rafe by the neck, they threw him to the ground and started kicking him. We jumped up and tore at them trying to keep them from hurting our friend, but they shook us off and kept kicking him. When Rafe started vomiting blood they stopped and turned their attention to us. We were dragged into the woods and raped over and over again. They took turns with each of us, our fight was gone, they had won again."

"Rafe died there in that beautiful place with the sun smiling down and the breeze of God's breath lifting his tortured soul home. Oh I didn't feel that way at first I just wanted to kill those bastards, cut them up in little pieces and send them home to their families. Later as I thought about it, the more I knew that if we did that then we would have turned into the animals like them, they would have truly won. The more I learned to forgive the more I saw Rafe's face smiling at me. I knew he was at peace now something he hadn't ever had while he was here. He'd had the double whammy of being a man lover and black."

"Me and Miss Emma, two young girls raped, beaten, sore from the inhuman violence and shamed by our living through it, made our way back to town and went to the city fathers to complain about the attack. We were told, we had made the mistake of leaving the safety of the town and they weren't willing to start a war with the white people in the next town over us three foolish people who had broken the rules. Well now, I decided it didn't matter where you live, you never are really and truly free!"

"I stopped at Tommy John's shack to see if there was any news of Edward. I had wanted to go sooner but still didn't trust myself. The pull of liquor is real strong even now.

"When Tommy John saw me he grinned that evil grin as though he was happy about the bad news he was about to deliver.

"Well now ya done it," he said, "ya killed Edward and Miz Flossy can't dance with broken legs so ya got yer way at last."

"What in hell are you saying? I screamed at him.

"You ain't heard the news yet? Edward was drunk and wading in a pond to trying to catch a fish when he slipped and hungry gators are pretty fast. Miz Flossy went in after him and was hit by the thrashing tail. She managed to pull herself out by grabbing a low hanging branch. She had the privilege of watching her lover eaten by gators. So you see if ya hadn't drove him out to the swamps he would be here drinking booze instead of gator shit. It's all yer fault!"

"I felt so guilty, Tommy John was right. I had driven Edward to his death; my handsome Edward would never laugh, dance, or love again. I went back to my room and thought more about leaving. Could I outrun my feelings of blame, I didn't know but I had to try.

"In those days I felt guilty about the fact that I had helped kill Edward but a few years later I knew that I could never have done such a thing. Bad things turn into good things sometimes. If Edward hadn't run from me with that bitch, God knows where I would have ended up. I had to believe that so I could get on with the rest of my life."

Jessie's eyes filled with tears again but this time there was no torment in them. I slid over to the edge of her bed and took her in my arms and held her until we both stopped crying. We both had needed that cleansing of the soul and Jessie was ready to relate the rest of her story. I wanted desperately to hear how she tore herself out of that quagmire of hate and escaped to her new life, but I didn't want her to become too tired. She asked for a taste of water and then began again.

"It sounds like all I had were bad times doesn't it?" After much thought she added, "but there were a lot of good times too."

"By now you know how I loved to cook and thanks to Sophia I was good at it. That was what I was going to do. What a perfect way to make my way in this old world. I was working up the guts to tell my friend Miz Emma I was leaving town, when she beat me to the punch and told me she was marrying a drifter who had sold her the piano that stood in the parlor. They were going to be on the road most of the time so she wouldn't have much time for me. That told me that I was doing the right thing. I made up my mind and left the town and safety that very night."

"I moved by night and slept by day, oh I was some kind of animal during those lost days. I stole food, milked farmer's cows for milk and slowly made my way toward what I hoped was north. Follow the handle, was the song we sung when I was a child and it stuck in my head. A few times I watched as black folk went passing by but I was too afraid to let them see me cause look what happened with Master David. He was black just like us but he was raised white and thought we were below him. The others working on his place had called him an uppity nigger and he did act more white than black.

"New folks that I met expected to hear me talk like they had heard other black folks talk, so that is just what I did. By the time I met you folks I was set in my ways and I wasn't ready to change again."

"After being in the household long enough to learn trust, I thought about letting you folks know that I wasn't just an uneducated slave, but I wasn't ready to answer a lot of questions from the people I was beginning to love. The time slipped by and I decided to keep the secret.

"The last few years were good ones, but it didn't start out that way. It was Eighteen Ninety Nine; I was twenty-five years old, no family, and no job. The southern farmers wouldn't hire a black woman to cook for them; they were lucky if they had enough food for themselves, besides they couldn't take a chance on having a slave on their property. There were bands of criminals out grabbing black folks off the roads and turning them in for a reward, be they free or not. Their free papers would get lost or burnt. When they run them down they always beat them for running. If they couldn't find an owner we heard that they even hung some.

"I was beat down from hunger and almost ready to give myself up to what ever anybody wanted to do to me. I heard some voices talking as they passed the place where I was hiding waiting for the night to come when I could move on. I could tell they were white by the way they talked and I still wasn't quite ready to give up, so I listened. They were talking about a preacher man that had hit their town and was saving folks from the gout, the chill blains and just about any other ailment that came down the pike. Could it be my friend John Cavendish? Dare I go closer to town and see for myself? Damned right I have to go, I told myself, What other choice have I got? This is my last chance at freedom! When the voices moved off I followed the path they had taken, trying to stay in the scrub brush along the side of the road. The sounds of their foot steps led me to an open space where a wagon stood, on the side of the wooden cover was painted the words, Save Your Soul From Hell! And in smaller letters below was written these words, Preacher John Cavendish Can Help.

Would he remember me, after all it had been many years and we both had changed.

"Waiting for the men to buy the magic elixir and leave was pure hell for me, so close, yet so far from safety and all the men were in a talkative mood including John Cavendish. He was in good voice and as I listened it took me back the years we had traveled together. I knew then that he would help me, I just knew.

" I sat in the weeds as they traded stories about life and their heroic captures of runaway slaves, not knowing that they were talking to a man who hated slavery as much as the slaves did.

"When the elixir finally hit them they staggered off to their homes and bed, I called out to John Cavendish. " Is it alright if I come out now, and is it safe for me to come to the wagon?"

"My God is that you Jessie? I been looking for you all over this Gods green earth, where in the hell have you been?"

"Well let me tell you my heart sang. I was safe for a while."

Jessie was getting so weak, but she had to get her history off her mind, until she did that she could not rest. I think it was her way of saying, that she didn't want us to forget that she was here and she did leave a mark on this earth.

Her cotton nightdress was wet with sweat, but still she shook from the creeping final cold that threatened her body and soul. I knew she would live on in the hearts of her friends and family, but I could not tell her that until the very end. My hopeful heart would not let me. Oh I knew she was dying, but when it's someone you love, you pray for miracles.

After bathing her and putting on a fresh, dry cotton gown, I teased her about wearing cotton when she could afford the best that money could buy.

She whispered, "I remember where I came from. I remember my roots."

# Chapter Ten

Jessie slept for a few hours but I couldn't. I was remembering what she had told me of her roots and realized how fortunate we were to have her come into our lives. I came to the conclusion that we were destined from the beginnings of time to become a part of each other's lives. She was the levelheaded one in our loose knit family at Haven Place, beautiful girls and wealthy men coming and going, fabulous parties given whenever Kate or Jessie had a need for a bash.

Jessie ruled the kitchen and when she was in a cooking frenzy, it seemed like she wanted the whole world to sample her food.

Kate had given her free rein when ever possible because Jessie was not only the best cook in town, but she also had most of the male clients intimidated which meant that Kate felt more secure with her there. Jessie began to stir around in bed so I knew that I was about to here more of her story.

She opened her eyes and stared blankly at me. I could see the recognition begin to flash in her eyes as she came back from where ever it was that her dreams had flown to.

"Now where was I" Jessie continued, "Oh yes, "When John Cavendish accepted me with open arms and gave me food and a place to rest, I knew I was safe for the moment. I slept for almost two days without waking. John Cavendish was growing worried and finally woke me at dusk of the second day with a bowl of soup and a chunk of sourdough bread. I had forgotten how hard trail bread is until John Cavendish reminded me to soak the bread in the soup. I ate like there was no tomorrow, and who knew maybe there wouldn't be?

"I traveled with him for the next three months slowly working our way north, John Cavendish had promised me he would get me to a safe place in the free states before he left again.

"I got the travel bug and it won't let me be," John Cavendish explained, "'sides the South is the only place I know and I ain't getting any younger. It's a hard life I chose but it's the only life I know. It has given me a meager living and a chance to meet many interesting people. Some good and some bad but I never tried to judge them, that's Gods job. Speaking of God, I hope to join him and when I do I want to die in the South. It's my home."

"When we reached the Ohio border John Cavendish took me to little white clapboard house setting right next to the railroad tracks. I wondered how they could keep the house so white with all the soot and grim that the locomotive spewed from its stack. I soon found out!

"John Cavendish went to the door and knocked. A little old black lady in a nightgown and robe opened the door. She was bare foot and I could see the soot embedded in her toenails. It made me sick to see those dirty feet but I soon learned why her toes were so filthy."

"John asked a woman named Frieda, can you help? I got a gal here that needs to get to a safe place as soon as possible,

"I can if she can work for room and board, this house needs scrubbing every other day and I can't do it alone. Told Old Fred I wanted a white house with flowers in the yard when I married him, well he got me the house but in the only place that we were allowed to build. This house setting right next to the tracks has made my life a living hell. That dammed Fred died after five years of marriage leaving me to do it all! The dammed flowers wouldn't grow but I still got my white house. It takes a heap of doing but it goes a lot faster when I have my nieces come and help. Niece, what the hell is your name in case anybody should ask?"

"I told her that my name was Jessie, and I was used to hard work."

"We'll see about that, the old women spat out. "If you can you work extra hard and help keep this old house white then your welcome to stay till I can get in touch with friends further on North. They still come this far to find runaways and I don't want to get caught either, who would keep my house white?"

"I decided right then that she was a little tetched in the head but she was a safe harbor for this child who was on the run.

"It seemed like I was running all my life and the only time I ever looked back was when I thought of Edward King. He was a chaser but he made my blood boil from wanting him. I hear everybody has that feeling about their first love, but I swear to God my feelings for Edward King were different."

"After eating a meager meal of grits and greens, John Cavendish took my hand and we went out to his home on wheels and there he gave me a hand full of coins, kissed my forehead, and pulling himself up to the seat where we had spent many an day riding from town to town, he gave the horse a gentle tap with the whip and drove off toward another town and his adventures in life. I watched to see if he would look back, but he never did. Again, the misery of being alone gnawed at my gut."

Jessie asked me if I had ever eaten hot sourdough bread fried in bacon fat while sitting by a campfire. Had I ever watched the stars signaling for you to follow, and listen to the night things singing their songs of praise?

"Can you imagine that," she asked, "singing praises to a God who had created them to crawl on the earth their whole lives?"

"You know Lorie, I never had a drink of ice cold water until I was cooking for Miss Kate, Water don't stay cold when it is stored in a wooden keg, but it slakes the thirst anyway."

She's getting delirious, I thought, as Jessie rambled on about the small things that had impressed her throughout her life. Jessie began her story again.

"I stayed with Frieda, until the next visitor came. That was just long enough to collect the soot of many a train. The black tar was everywhere. My toenails, fingernails, and ever wrinkle on my body was stained with the dirt from the engines hauling folks to their beginnings or endings. Frieda and I would bath each night and then she would sit in the living area of the two room white house and dig at the black stains under her fingernails. How hopeless I thought, she spends her time digging the stain away each night and then goes out the next day and puts her hands in the water that stains them black again. I was sure those stains were there for the rest of her life, she was wasting her time, but later in life I realized that is all she wanted. This was her life's rhythm and that rhythm is what kept her going.

"The day of my independence came was the day the stern faced man driving a small covered wagon drove up to the soot stained house. A stern faced woman sat on the seat next to him. They smiled at me with an effort to seem friendly as they came nearer. Their mouths stretched into thin little lines of greeting as they came right up to the house where we were scrubbing. A passel of children was peeping out the open flaps of the canvas tent. They all were white and grinning directly at me, my heart dropped into my guts. Here I was waiting for someone to help me escape and along comes this pasty white family smiling and showing teeth that seemed as though they were ready to tear me to pieces."

"Frieda ignored them until the man stepped down from the wagon and came close to the house where we were washing dirt from her not quite white home. It had been washed too many times and was in need of a fresh coat of white wash."

Jessie paused in her tale to look back into the past and reflect on the women's passion for her white house.

"Can't really blame her for hanging on to her dream, it was all she ever had to hang onto. I watched to see what this man with the grinning face was about to do next. Too many years of hiding and being chased by white men had made me edgy with all strangers.

"These white folks and their strange way of dressing made me nervous. Him in his black coat and black wide brimmed hat and her with her black dress and little white snood sitting on her head. The children that hung out the tent that covered their wagon were dressed the same as the man and women except for the women's snood. The girls wore bonnets. I never saw anyone as dressed up except for when we was going to church meetings."

"He said, howdy friend, we are here to help you. My wife, family and I are all heading north and we got word that you needed a ride. We have prayed about this and God has instructed us to come to your aid. Are you ready to travel with us?

"I looked at the old women and she just nodded her head."

"Don't worry about washing the house today, another niece will be along shortly and she can help me clean that damn soot offen this place."

"But won't the white folks notice a the difference, a strange girl claiming to be your niece?" I asked

"Naw, we all look the same to them white folks." Frieda chuckled.

"She was one brave lady, never did hear how she came about passing runaways through her house like a stream through rough country."

"When they finally convinced me that Frieda would be alright I joined the children in the wagon. I had to stay hidden cause the roads were watched all the time. We traveled during the day and only stopped to pray, eat and bath. Often the children got out to run alongside the wagon or to go into the bushes for their daily duty and when it took too long, Mary, the mother, would drop off and wait for the child to finish. That family really loved and cared for their children.

"Why did they put their family in danger helping slaves to escape, I wondered, so I asked."

"My child," answered the father, David by name, "we believe that all men are brothers and we wouldn't make our brother a slave so why would we allow another human being to be treated worse then animals. When we see the need we must do something to help, this we have taught our children. If we don't help our brothers and sisters then we have shone our children that these are only words. We must be true to our faith."

"My private times came in the dark of night when I could slip out of camp and squat behind a bush or tree with lots of leaves or long grass to help me stay clean. I didn't drink water very often during the day because I would have to come out of the tent to relieve myself and it wasn't safe to do that yet. It was hard not to think about peeing during the day, but it was easier then hanging from a tree."

"We finally got to the state of Ohio where the family had a piece of land waiting for them. Other friends had gone on ahead and settled on farms in a green valley called Greenville. They had staked out a piece of land for this family too, and that is how I got out of the South."

"The neighbors greeted the family with a house raising and food was prepared by women who were all dressed just like Mary. The children all looked alike, blond hair blue eyed and very serious little faces. I thought back to when I was younger and remembered the smiling faces of the other children that I had lived with. Even after a hard day in the fields they had joy in their lives, these white children didn't."

"When it came time I told the family that I needed to leave. I guess the travel bug had bitten me too cause there was this desperate need to move on. It seemed as if I was always searching for something, but I didn't know what. The family asked me to stay with them, but I was still scared, and they were white folks. I didn't know what they would do if a posse of white men came looking for runaways, turn me over or die protecting me so I left the safety of the farm."

"I packed up my few belongings and said goodbye to those friendly folks and was on my way into a strange new future.

"I still traveled mostly after dark cause I still didn't feel that I was safe this close to the South. I had heard stories of black folks disappearing off the streets of the next town over and I hadn't gotten this far to be dragged back to that hellhole again.

"While traveling on the road just a little after dusk I saw a wagon headed in my direction and I tried to blend into the trees at the edge of the road, but it didn't work."

"That is when I met Joshua, he was driving a team of horses pulling a wagon loaded down with lumber and tools. His soothing voice was tenderly consoling the beasts that were pulling that heavy load in the heat of the day. The steady cadence of the horses told me they trusted this man.

"Girl" he shouted, "you ain't hiding from nobody in those trees, you stand out like a black bear in a field of white cotton. Want a lift to town?"

"Pretending that I was just interested, I asked, what town is next and is it to the north?"

"You a runaway?" Demanded the man, all the while looking all funny eyed at me.

"I ain't no runaway, I'm a free women, but I need to get North to join my family." I lied but that was alright cause he was a stranger and I didn't owe him the truth."

"Girl, you hop up here if you want a ride to town. You got anywhere to stay when you get there? I can put you up for the night in case you ain't got no kin to go to."

"What about your wife," I asked, "Ain't she got something to say about it?"

"Ain't got a wife nor child but sure would like to have both to share my good fortune with."

"Well, I could use a place to stay but just for the night. I am not going to put up with no funny business. If I stay its got to be understood that we share house for the night and that's all."

"Don't you worry little miss, I got plenty of young gals waiting for just a look from me but I been too busy working and saving to buy property and build a barn to think of settling down with one woman. By the way the barn is where I sleep until I get the house built."

"There he sat all full of himself, bragging to this child of God like he was right up there with our Maker. I decided right then and there that I would stay at his place and see if he really was as rich as he said. Joshua, Joshua Baker, was his name, didn't tell a lie about sleeping in the barn and he did own a sixty-acre piece of land. He had a small section of the barn portioned off like a house. I offered to do the cooking and cleaning but he said no he had Jenny to do that chore. After I was there for a day I found out why, She was not his live in women but she only came every day to cook, clean and wash his clothes. He was kind and gentle to Jenny who needed the job so badly that she would have done anything he asked.

"When Joshua first introduced us all she did was bob her head and wiping her wet hands on her apron, offered her right one and smiled a small smile at me. I could see the fear in her eyes; she thought I was there to take her job.

"After she had left for the day Joshua told me that he could do all those chores himself but she needed the work to live and support her family. Her husband had been whipped so badly by a crazy master that he couldn't work

*JESSIE'S FLIGHT TO FREEDOM*

but he could take care of the children until she got home. She always made meals ahead of time so that he could feed the three children their lunch and put them down for a nap in the afternoon so he could rest too. They lived in a shack far enough down wind from the barn that the smell of the few cows Joshua had in there didn't pass their fragrance into the shacks open windows. We smelled it but they didn't."

"Jenny was happy I didn't push her out of her job, and that I was content to work outside. Building myself worth went right along with the raising of the beams that was the beginning of the simple house that Joshua was building. Building a safe life instead of letting other folks demolish my dreams became just as important to me. I stayed with Joshua for eight years. I was his woman. We had it pretty good, nobody to bother us and we worked hard and slept like babies at night.

"Jenny kept doing her cooking and cleaning until one morning a couple of years after I settled there she showed up with all three of her children, her face was hard and her eyes were filled with grief but she wasn't looking for sympathy, she just wanted to collect her wages so she could move on. It seems that her husband Ben had died during the night and she had the children had buried him in the meadow behind her shack. Joshua took the grief stricken woman into his arms and tried to soothe her pent up grief. When she was able to understand what he was promising she let out a shout of hallelujah and told the children"

"We don't have to leave we are home to stay." From then on the children came to work with Jenny everyday. They were a joy to watch as they played and enjoyed running around outside, something they hadn't done before. Ben had been a good father but he worried if the children were not in his sight so he had kept them in the house for all the time that Jenny was gone off to work. They seldom saw the day in full bloom it was either daybreak or dusk when they could escape to the meadow where they could have a true sense of freedom."

"I helped Joshua build the house, farm the land and I shared his bed. I was content to stay for a little longer but when the house was finally done he asked me to marry up with him. I wasn't against marriage but I wasn't ready to make that place my home. I knew in my gut that out there was someone and someplace where I really belonged. Those were some of the good days. You know I can't even remember what Joshua looked like, all I remember about him was he was a kind man. I later heard that he hitched up with Jenny and raised her three children plus one they had together. That's the way it should have worked, they were supposed to be together. If I would've stayed it would not have worked out for them or me."

Jessie was becoming so weak that I didn't want her to finish her story and when I suggested that she rest and have some broth to build up her strength she said okay.

Trying to hide the pain she gave me a wan smile and said, "But I am not going to sleep, sleep is too much like death."

# Chapter Eleven

Evidently Jessie who had always been clean and tidy couldn't smell it but her wasting body had taken on an odor. I bathed her often and did my best to keep her smelling fresh and clean. I had the boys go out to the pharmacy and get me some more of the lilac and rose scented waters that she had always used when she bathed herself. I used it generously each time I cleaned her body. I had gotten used to the smell of Lilacs and swore when this was over I would never buy the flowers or the scented water again. When I finished her bath this morning I took a long look at her tiny wrinkled face and prayed that she would not have long to suffer. She let me feed her a couple of spoonful of the broth, and then she turned her head signaling that she was done eating, I straightened her bed while she lay remembering better times. When I finished straightening her quilt that Sadie had given her she was ready to begin again.

Touching her cold gray hand I gently rubbed it and made her promise to let me know when she was too tired to go on even though I knew she couldn't stop until she had reached her goal. She had grown restless, filled to overflowing with the good memories that she wanted to live on even after she had gone. She needed to talk and I needed to listen.

"Lorrie have you ever loved someone so deeply that you could still feel their arms around you. Holding and touching you in those intimate places that he knew would start the fire of passion? When I lost Edward my heart grew empty, gone was the love of life. I could never be complete. I was like a puzzle with a piece missing. My heart turned to ice and that ice protected me for a long time after Edward died. I went through each day as though it were the last day of my life, until I met Joshua. He taught me to care about him and the people who came into our lives. I didn't want to start caring about him but the warmth of Joshua's generous heart melted the ice. It was never passion but it was a comfort to me when I needed it most. I lived and laughed but never with any real joy. I was always in the background watching myself. Pretending to take pleasure in life but I was still on the outside looking in."

"When Joshua asked me to marry him I thought a long time about accepting, but my gut told me that I would be losing my last chance of finding my place in this world. I had to say no.

"Times were different now, I could travel in daylight but I never lost the fear of traveling when white folks could see me. I always had the feeling that the posse was ready to jump out and grab me, haul my black ass back south and hang me for a runaway."

"I had a hard time saying goodbye to the man who took me in and cared for me. He taught me so much and he even tried to get me to talk like the white folks, but I still didn't trust him enough to tell him that I could talk any other way. I kept talking the way the slaves did when they didn't want white folks to figure out what they were truly saying. Add an s or change the t to a d to every other word and it becomes a code. It was just another way of showing disrespect for the white man's way, a small way of fighting back. It kept us from going crazy.

"I never did have much respect for white folks until I met Harrison and the rest of the gals at Haven Place. John Cavendish, Harrison, and Francis St. James were the first and only white men that I ever really trusted and that trust took some time in coming."

Jessie sunk into a peaceful silence, her eyes were open but she wasn't in that old tired body, she had gone back to a sweeter, better time. I waited by her side until her soul came back and slipped into the tired old body that was lying on this bed of pain. I didn't stir, I couldn't disturb the serenity of her lingering dream, and I had to let her savor the peace of the moment without my straightening the rumpled quilt or her nightgown. The sweat would just have to stay on her brow until she was fully back into the agonizing distress of her present life. The calm way she turned her eyes and looked at me I knew she now possessed the strength to go on with her story.

The smile Jessie gave me was as close as she could get to her old self and for a moment my hopes soared. Then the truth descended on my heart, she was in the last throes of death. I had to let her go when she was ready. I must hear her story, let her exhaust herself if need be, she had a passion to finish the story of her life and nothing must get in the way.

"Lorrie, those first few days traveling on the train was pure hell, white folks staring at you, whispering to each other, and those slick carpetbaggers looking at you like you were a piece of meat on the auction block. I kept my eyes staring straight ahead and prayed that we would get to Pennsylvania soon. When I got off that train I felt the earth lift off my shoulders!

*JESSIE'S FLIGHT TO FREEDOM*

"Joshua had given me enough for train fare to Pennsylvania and he had given me a woman's name, Thelma, and her address. He said she would help me get settled when I got there. Well Thelma did try to help, but her idea of getting along was far different from mine. She had a room in a sleazy hotel run by a white man, but he catered only to blacks. He could charge double the going rate and who was there to complain to? He also made it a habit of dropping in whenever he felt like it, using her for his pleasure. She wasn't a whore, she worked as a maid for a rich white family, but she allowed him to make use of her because he charged her less then the others and she had nowhere else to go. She didn't make enough money to move and she was a timid little girl child, not used to taking care of herself.

"After seeing her situation I knew that I couldn't live like that. I had done some pretty wicked things in my life but sleeping with that beast was not going to be another one of my sins.

"I stayed with Thelma for two days and after posting a sign on the building of the local grocery store I found a job cooking for the sheriff's household. He had seen my poster that was nailed to the shattered wooden frame edge of the doorway. The poster had almost hit him in the face when he opened the door of the grocery shop to buy food for his family. He came to the hotel looking for me and asked me if I was a good cook and I answered, "I ain't had no grumbling so far."

"Sheriff Chase was his name and when he had introduced himself to me I had to chuckle to myself, he was the last man I could picture chasing anyone. He wore his trousers belted just below his sizable paunch, and he was constantly hitching them up as he talked. If he had worn suspenders they might have help but then his gut was so huge that I'm not sure he could find suspenders large enough to fit him

"He nodded and asked, "Would I like to have the job of cooking for his family? He explained that his wife was ailing and unable to keep house and cook the meals too. He glanced around the shabby room and I could almost read his thoughts. *Do I want to hire this person if she is willing to live in this hovel?*

"I made it plain to him that I had only arrived in town a few days ago and was looking for improved living conditions.

"When I opened my mouth, and out came the black folks talk that he was expecting, I could see his body relax. This is what he was expecting, a black woman, far from home and defenseless, someone who he could take advantage of.

"Over the years I had taken on a lot of weight, I had rounded out and I was satisfied with my body. Joshua had liked my ample body, he said I was full and firm, a woman a fella could hold on to.

"When the sheriff's wife saw me she smiled and welcomed me into their home, her eyes told me that I would not be a threat, she knew I wouldn't be tempting her husband to bed me. Mrs. Chase showed me the room I was to use and instructed me as to their schedule. The evening meal was to be served at seven every evening except Sunday, and then the main meal was at three. As a Christian family they and their three children spent the rest of the day in evening prayers. I worked for the sheriff and his family for seven years. They liked my cooking and I liked the fact that after a week of good meals he had given me a dollar a month raise. Oh, I know it don't sound like much now but in those days it was good money.

"The children were good little people, but always sad eyed. They loved their mother and she was always too weak to play with them or take them to the many events that happened around that growing city. There were church picnics which were held in the local cemeteries where it was always well kept up and very peaceful, the county fair was a big thing for the children and of course the traveling tent revival. A white preacher came to town and shouted at these Christian folks telling them they were going to hell and they paid him money for that. They were always passing the hat at those things.

"When my friend Thelma and me went to prayer meetings we sang praises to God. Our minister told us about the promise land where the streets were paved with gold and we were free like everybody else. We came away filled with hope, not shame like the white folks. I was kind of glad when that preacher told them white folks that they were going to hell when they died, cause they sure made our lives hell here on earth."

"In that fifth year just before spring Mrs. fell gravely sick. She couldn't stop coughing; her face would turn purple just trying to catch her breath. The doctor said that Mrs. Chase had a lung disease. He called it Tuberculoses, and said there wasn't any cure. We had to keep the children away as it was easily spread. Sheriff Chase asked the doctor and he said that it was in the last stages and it shouldn't be too long before she died. Sheriff Chase kept away from her too so it was just me to tend to her needs. Why I didn't catch it I will never know, but now that I think about it maybe God had other plans for me. Maybe he felt it was my turn to find friends and family to share my life.

"After the funeral for Mrs. Chase, which I might add, was very small funeral being as the town folks were still leery of catching TB, I took my duds, the money that I had saved and hit for New York. I had heard that the color of your skin didn't matter much in New York City and if that were so then that is where I wanted to be.

"When the train arrived in the station we, the black folks had to wait until the white folks were off the train. Then we were allowed to get off enter the train station to freshen up but we were not allowed enter the station. We were herded to the end of the platform and were told by the conductor, to get the hell out of here! Well so much for the stories I had heard!"

"I had just gotten off the platform when this handsome white man asked, "Is there anyone in this crowd that can cook for a large group of people, and if so are you looking for work?"

"I had had my fill of working for the white folks but I needed work and so I raised my arm. Two other women in the crowd raised their arms too; I was bigger and meaner looking and my malicious dirty looks caused them to slowly lower their arms. I was the only one left with my arm raised.

The white man who had asked the question introduced himself as Harrison and explained that his friend had a house ill repute called Kate's Place and she needed a cook. Are you still willing to work for us?

"I was the last person to be judging these people, and this job would only be until I found something else.

"I gotta have the run of the kitchen, don't nobody set foot in my kitchen lessen I say so." I was still talking like folks expected any low no account nigra to talk and that talk had helped me so far, so I continued to use it.

"He said, I had myself deal and he took my hand and shook it like I was someone special.

"Giving me a note with instructions on how to find Kate's place, that trusting fool gave me a little money to grab some food to fill my hungry gut, then he smiled and said, he would see me tomorrow

"Oh, I thought about not showing up for work, but I had given him my word and I still needed a place to stay. Best damn thing I ever did in my life! Showing up at Kate's whorehouse changed my whole world.

"I searched around town for a room stay the night but no one wanted to rent to a black woman hauling a ruck sack with all her goods in it. When it got too late to search further I headed for this whore house called Kate's Place.

"I'm sure you can guess the reaction I got when I showed up on Kate's doorstep at the darkest hour before dawn. Lady that she was, she welcomed me with grace and charm even though she was scared half to death.

"Imagine if you will a black woman twice your size standing on your stoop at that hour in the morning. When she lifted the candle her eyes grew big and she later told me that she had almost peed her pants, but she was gracious enough to hide her surprise and fear and welcomed me into her home. What a women she was!" Jessie paused and then added, "She deserved better than what she got. She left us way too soon."

"White folks had never treated me as an equal in a long and that takes some getting used to, but all the girls followed Kate's lead and I was accepted into the only real home I had ever known."

Jessie's hands shook as she wiped away a tear and stared at the ceiling. Her mind had gone back to better, happier days, and I was happy for her temporary escape from the agonizing pain of the tumor that was stealing the life from her body. After resting for a few minutes she opened wide her eyes filled with pain and continued.

"You know the first time I met Sadie, I knew in my heart she was the daughter I never had. Her down-to-earth simplicity captured my heart. Oh, she learned to give back what she received, but she did it in such a way that even her worst enemy had to admire her. She was such a sweet child when I first met her and even with all the heartbreak that happened, she never really changed.

"Did you know that the all the people at Haven Place always thought I hired some one to kill John, Sadie's first husband, but I didn't? Oh, I'll admit I hired Zeb, a huge black man from the bottoms to beat the snot out of John, but before he had a chance to carry out his mission some mugger beat him to it. I think Zeb knew who did the deed but refused to tell me the mugger's name. I guess you could say that John was destined to die that way and it didn't matter who did it.

"I never denied the suspicions that other folks had of me; I felt that if they thought that I could hire someone to kill another human being they would watch their step around me and mine. It kept quite a few folks in line."

"When I first found out about the cancer I was all tore up inside, I cried a couple of days, refused to eat but my stomach kept giving off the terrible growling sound of hunger. It was embarrassing. Then I got so damned mad at the lord above, I ranted and raved at a God who would permit me to find home and family after long, hard years only to turn around and tear it all away. Finally I realized that none of that whining was going to help. I filled what time I had left with important things that would last long after I was gone. I contacted Francis St. James, you remember him, the rutting pig with the cud under his lower lip, well he gave up chewing a few years later and was actually pleasant to be around. Liked the man hated the habit!

"After I made out my will giving the boys a goodly chunk of money and all of my friends a little gift to remember me by I left the bulk of my estate to my little Sadie. Imagine that! A black runaway slave having an estate to leave to her family."

"Lorrie I'm getting a bit tired now. I think I'll close my eyes for a little bit, maybe this pain will go away."

Jessie never woke from her nap. The last thing I heard from the motionless Jessie were these words. "Yes Edward I'm coming."

My friend Jessie died, as I had known her, bravely, with grace and dignity.

Jessie had made us promise to keep the funeral small, only her boys, Seth and Samuel, my husband Evan, Francis St. James and myself.

She didn't want anyone else to know about her passing, it would only cause more pain for her other friends at this unfortunate time.

The year was nineteen thirty-one and most of the banks had failed two years earlier. Times were desperate and the majority of Jessie's friends had lost their life savings. Newspapers carried stories of some of the very wealthy men who had resorted to taking their own lives. I guess failing was too much for many of the successful, influential men to swallow. They leaped out windows, and many used guns to stamp out their shame.

We laid Jessie out in a soft blue dress sprinkled with small white flowers, her hands were folded across her small breast and her feet were sporting gay red shoes. She loved red shoes. She said they always reminded her of Edward King and the many nights the two of them had spent dancing in the moonlight. His arms wrapped around her and their bodies pressed tight against each other.

She had died with Edward King in her heart and mind. He had been dead for forty-five years and still she carried her love of him into death. I only hoped that he was waiting to welcome her on the other side. She had been loyal with her love for him as long as she had lived and justly deserved a reunion with him in the here after.

Francis St. James processed her will and notified the other recipients of her sizable fortune.

The other folks and I, who had attended Jessie's funeral, were anxious to have a reunion with Sadie, and her children.

Evan and I stayed in Jessie's spacious apartment and were soon joined by Philip, Cathy, and Rachael. It was a lovely apartment that Jessie had lived in all the years that she had owned the restaurant. Jessie had bought the whole block as soon as she could afford it. Her intentions of never being kicked out of her home again kept her mind clear and at peace with the world. She had a home, friends, and most of all she had family.

Seth and Samuel loved the fact that they would have someone with which to share their grief and they waited on us hand and foot.

When Francis called and told us that Sadie was in New York, we were all thrilled to see our friend again and exchange our life stories with each other. Even though we talked every single week since we all went our separate ways, there are some things that cannot be shared on the telephone.

Going quickly into the bathroom I checked myself in the mirror, a few lines were sprinkled across my face, my blond hair was more silver than gold and my figure wasn't as slim as it used to be, but I had been looking at this face for many years and had become accustomed to the changes, would Sadie even begin to recognize me?

Evan instinctively knew what I was thinking, following me down the hall and peeking through the open door he declared, "Lorrie darling we all have changed over the years but you have only grown more beautiful."

God bless his soul, he always knew what to say to sooth my worried feelings.

I teased my husband right back, as we have always done when either of us are sad. "You're prejudice my sweet Evan, but we do have a wonderful marriage and a wonderful child so that makes growing old worth while. I do hope the Stewart's are having an easy time with Sid, you know how she gets sometime."

"Lorrie my dear, don't you worry about Sid she may be a little hard headed at times but she is a gentle loving child and won't give the Stewart's a hard time."

"Evan, she's only sixteen years old and I still worry about her!" After pausing for a moment I added, "she is still my baby girl and will always be."

"I know my dear, but we are going to have to think about letting her have more freedom. She is growing into a woman and must find a way of life for herself. I suggest the loveliest lady I know get herself ready to meet an old friend. I know that dear friend Sadie, will be delighted to see you and all her other friends from the past."

Patting down stray hairs from my new marceled cut and straightening my rumpled skirt and hoping to create a lighter mood I swung my pink and green beads in a circle over my breast and announced, "Twenty three skidoo, I love you! Now lets go and surprise Sadie."

Even though I was exhausted from the long days and nights spent with Jessie I was also excited about seeing Sadie and her boys.

Off we went to the hotel where our friend Sadie had spent the night.

I had the desk clerk call her room and I teased her by saying, "Guess who this is." I hate it when other people do that to me, as I'm always afraid that I will guess wrong and hurt someone's feelings.

"I recognize the voice," she answered, "but how can that be that voice belongs to my friend Lorrie and she is in Buffalo?"

Filled with excitement Evan, Philip, Cathy, Rachael and I climbed the stairs, walking to Sadie's room. Filled with schoolgirl anticipation Cathy, Rachael and I giggled and then shushed each other while Evan only shook his head at our schoolgirl antics. Her room was at the end of the hall and when we knocked she answered immediately.

The meeting was wonderful but I could read the puzzlement in Sadie's eyes. She stared at the group of people waiting outside her door as recognition came slowly. She too had forgotten that we all have grown older even though we don't realize it.

Her memorable beauty had been unscathed by the passage of time. The precise youthful curve of Sadie's face had slowly merged over the years, softening the marks left by her life experiences. She had developed into a lovely mature woman.

Her eyes reflected her joy at seeing and us my heart sang. Here was the Sadie I knew, full of life and with a smile that could light a city.

She explained that the twins, James and Jonathon, didn't come with her because she didn't have enough train fare to bring them. She had left them with their sister, Katy; Katy's husband Jared and a house full of their children.

We took her back to Jessie's place and let her see the home Jessie had built for herself. We all relaxed in the tastefully, comfortable residence of our late friend Jessie. It seemed as though her spirit was there with us, and we knew we were welcome in her home. Sadie cried when she heard that Jessie didn't want her to suffer any more by being at her funeral. Jessie had wanted Sadie to remember her friend the way she had been.

When we were alone I asked Sadie about Marcus and she got this strange look in her eye. That look told me she still loved him even after all this time. I hoped that she would someday find peace with or without him.

Sadie and I sat on the now empty bed on which Jessie had died. I told Sadie parts of Jessie's story about her long, and harsh life, Sadie wept for her friend Jessie and her miserable life.

Why Jessie had always considered Sadie the child she never had still astonished Sadie. It still amazes me that all of the hell Jessie had been through, the disappointments, the abandonment, the degradation of her human spirit; she was still capable of love and loyalty.

After hearing just a small part of Jessie's story, we were all exhausted and ready for dinner and bed. We left Jessie's apartment and made our way to the New Deal Restaurant, Jessie's now famous eatery. She had named it after Mr. Roosevelt's plan for the economy.

Frances St. John, Jessie's lawyer and friend, had told me on one of his many visits to see Jessie, that she had left the New Deal Restaurant and a considerable amount of cash to her adopted child, Sadie. It seems Jessie had never believed in putting her money in banks. She said that white men ran banks and she still had a hard time trusting most white men.

Jessie's lawyer had stored her cash in his office safe for many years. He said that little favor had been a privilege. He was grateful for the honor of helping the women who had saved him from a lifetime of drunkenness and a slow painful death.

Jessie had left a legacy greater than mere money; she had left a family who would remember and pass on her story to their children, grandchildren, friends, and their friends. She has gone on to be a legend in a world where Jessie would live in the minds and hearts of her family. She would be missed by all those who knew her, loved her, and all those unfortunate folks who have missed knowing her.

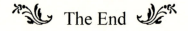

The End